war

Also by Todd Komarnicki

famine

Free

war

A NOVEL

TODD KOMARNICKI

ARCADE PUBLISHING • NEW YORK

FIRST EDITION

This is a work of fiction. Names, characters, places, and incidents are
either the work of the author's imagination or are used fictitiously.

Library of Congress Cataloging-in-Publication Data

Komarnicki, Todd.
  War : a novel / Todd Komarnicki. — 1st ed.
    p. cm.
  ISBN 978-1-55970-866-1 (alk. paper)
  1. Soldiers—Fiction. 2. Psychological fiction. I. Title.

  PS3561.O4523W37 2008
  813'.54—dc22   2007040366

Published in the United States by Arcade Publishing, Inc., New York
Distributed by Hachette Book Group USA

Visit our Web site at www.arcadepub.com

10 9 8 7 6 5 4 3 2 1

Designed by API

EB

PRINTED IN THE UNITED STATES OF AMERICA

For Jane

war

It wasn't supposed to happen. So soon. There are things I haven't learned yet. How long to look at the sea. The shape of a woman's back when she is slipping off her evening gown. The meaning of the Portuguese word *hoje*. It's probably so simple, but it felt tantalizing not knowing. Delicious, somehow. Not knowing meant there was always more to learn. That laziness and ignorance were finite. That I could decide to start paying attention at any moment.

Until now. Now, on the edge of this edgeless thing, I want to know every thing. I don't need their depth; the surface will suffice. The size of a sparrow's head. Why sleeping with socks makes the morning skin itch like ivy. When my brother stopped looking when he crossed the street. Great unknowns stack up around me. They hem me in with my own lack. Who wrote down the alphabet, the first time it was ever remembered. The depth of the deep end. The reason for sin.

What I do know is that they will come for me this morning. Between daybreak and the next bomb, there will be a hall full of footsteps, a thunder at the door. I have until then to decide how they will find me. Hanging like a ribbon. Piñataed on the avenue, sparing them the bother of the stairs. Sliced and splayed so they slip on my escape. Or like this. Alive. Waiting, as if I am not afraid. That would be my greatest lie of all.

When it began, I was a shipless port. My availability a seeming invitation. Sometimes all one must do to say yes is to not say no. Though I comprehended little of their designs, I was thrilled to have been chosen. Noticed. My waters muddied and hurried, my heart forced to beat to a rhythm besides my own breath. There was laughter in those days, and whiskey darker than a closed church. We drank like soldiers, pretending in our parentheses of safety that we were not soldiers ourselves.

Our commanding officer was married, his ring sunk deep into his knuckle like a saw left in a tree. He spoke of his spouse with grim appreciation. The marriage was a film he had once seen, a brilliant, disturbing film, but one he need not see again. We were reminded how lucky we were to have no one waiting and worrying for us at home. They preached loneliness as comfort and family as a soldier's millstone. Our lightness would help us survive. Children were discussed as utter folly. To have, desire, or recall. We behaved as if we had never been children ourselves, poised between birth and the grave in a hologram of community, distrust, and alcohol. We were handsome and whiskered and fucking necessary. Children were a cocoon. Men had wings. And the flailing and fluttering of them made me dizzy with flight.

The first man I killed was one of our own. It wasn't a plan. Not an initiation, not even a part of the training. It merely happened. Maybe he was young and pretending, drunk on Calvados and confusion, like I was. He hadn't seemed like a fresh recruit, a "bleeder" as they called me, the term being born of the way the unit cut us from our existing lives with such ferocity that we newbies were bleeders until we scarred over. Y. seemed like a veteran, scars and stories in equal measure. He wore his brown pants high, and a too-long belt that made him look both fat and skinny. Y. was also ripe with aftershave, a vestige from back in the days when he tried to hide his drinking from his girlfriend. We called him Aqua Velva. Or the older guys did. Velva, when they really wanted to piss him off. Anything impugning a comrade's manhood was both celebrated and feared, and this group of twelve, cloistered as we were, had become geniuses at it. These were our hallmarks. Comedy, cruelty, and silence. I learned about the third that Sunday. Some things happen and then are so quickly erased it's as if they never occurred at all. They exist only in the memory, like a stranger's lie or a half-remembered joke. Even violence can be cleaned

up, reduced to a filled-out report that gets promptly shredded. All this while I watched from the bar, still sticky with
his blood.

Y. was breaking bottles that night, or day, hard to tell, his
enemy unseen. A "future flashback," they called them, the
guarantee of seeing something so horrific in the future that
we had waking dreams about them in advance. Maybe he
wanted out, didn't have the courage that I am practicing
tonight. But he spun on me and my mumbled request for
him to shut the fuck up. Both his hands held bottle necks, no
bottles, the teeth of the remains glistening with foam. K.
tried to backsnatch him and caught a jigsaw worth thirty-
seven stitches across his unfortunate face.

When Y. rotated back toward me, my fist was already
traveling. Both his arms went slack, useless this close in. The
crack of his windpipe was like a body through glass. The
memory brings bile to this day . . . Why did I hit him so
perfectly? I hadn't thrown a hook since braces and monkey
bars. And here was this arrow of a punch, through the bull's-
eye. And why the throat? I knew I'd been wanting Y. to shut
up. L. and I were watching this or that game, and the an-
nouncer's nonsense had seemed more important than my
fellow man's woes. I don't believe I meant to kill him, but
even before he left K. bleeding and uglier, I hated him. I
wished he wasn't there. Didn't exist. And maybe that is the
same thing as wishing someone dead. Punch a man hard

enough, and that wish can come true. That's what I learned that day. And every day afterward. I learned we all longed for death. To provide it or abide in it. And the closer any one of us got, the deeper the brotherhood became.

"Grab a shower," R. said. And then he smiled, proud. I knew then that he'd been responsible for my allocation. Something blank and angry he had spotted in me, and he'd been right. I knew how to kill a man without rehearsal.

Y. wasn't replaced. We remained as eleven. We were never given orders, just told that they were pending. Our days were shapeless, the walls calendar-free. After a while, I stopped looking at my watch. Time bled by in fifths of booze. I never saw a delivery made, but every morning the bar had been restocked. We were fed when we got hungry, though a chef never materialized. Food on a plate and no washing up. We lived like spoiled children. Sans homework, sans responsibility. Except for The Run.

We called it The Run, though running was the least of it. The Run was an ever-changing, increasingly frightening obstacle course that had been fashioned from the hotel grounds. I couldn't say how often The Run go-code was slipped under our doors, but it felt like every day. And though I called it an obstacle course, it was more like a haunted house with all the lights on. Live ammo. But not in our weapons. Rubber bullets, Kevlar jackets, and speed were our only protection. The object was to get from the fountain outside the vestibule across the courtyard to the pool, up the fire escape, terrace to terrace, and onto the roof.

Whatever was shooting at us was designed to aim low. So L. took it in the ankle. K. continued his unlucky streak with a bullet to the shin. We needed full body armor, but R. said the only people who got shot were the ones who stopped. He was right. Motion was salvation. But where to move? In the interim between each Run, the landscape was altered, so our route of escape was never the same. Where there had been a gravel walkway was now a minilake of burning oil. The outdoor bar that once was last cover before the fire escape was next a shooting blind from which the enemy never ceased firing.

It took me eleven Runs to even see what the enemy looked like. On a day it rained, I slipped coming by the fountain, and the slip became a skid. I slid on my ass all the way behind the outdoor bar to face our attacker. It was R. himself.

He put a Glock to my head as his only word. I nodded comprehension, and he returned to his assault on the other nine men in his command. For a moment, I watched in awe. He will train us to be unkillable even if he must kill us on the way. I finally understood his full pleasure at my felling Y. I had done what he wasn't allowed to consummate.

I put my gun to his head. It was only rubber bullets, but, this close, it could put a tear in the temple big enough to end a man's journey. "Less," I said. This time, he nodded. Or I hoped he did, visioned it, and then I assed it out of there, across, over, and up onto the roof like a soul escaping from hell. R. and I never spoke of our exchange. But it did seem, despite the miasma of months we spent in the hotel, that less had been one request that had been honored.

The Run taught us how to be chased. The Shooting Gallery taught us how to hunt. Housed in what had been a string of hotel conference suites and ballrooms, the gallery was a lights on/lights off extravaganza of gunfire and staged surprise. Each of us took the gauntlet alone. We were given standard M4 carbines and a Beretta, the weapons we'd need in the field. The hallway was our path, and each room we passed was full of bogeymen.

The hypnotic cadence of electricity disallowed seeing exactly what these faux enemies were. Department-store mannequins? Crash-test dummies? Life-size dolls? They looked real enough so that when my bullets pierced what-ever their "flesh" was, it created both a sickening music and a rush of relief.

We were never given a score, only told that we were be-ing tested. And that every detail mattered. How many hits, how many misses, the speed with which we reloaded our clips. The guns we chose for each particular shoot. The way we learned the ever-changing patterns of attack. With each attempt, I could feel my eye growing keener, my heart calmer. I was preparing for something and was surprised to find it almost felt good.

The fact that all this came with a paycheck definitely was good. Biweekly bank deposits just as I'd been promised at recruitment. I was twenty-seven, living in a luxury hotel, albeit abandoned and half destroyed from the bombing, but once five-star, big beds, working sauna. I was eating and drinking until puking or passout for free. There was male friendship and television sports, even if they were only DVDs of long-ago contests. We still cheered as if we didn't know how it all ended. It helped allay the frustration of having our lives stuck on pause. And no rules, outside of The Run. This wasn't a setup worthy of a grievance. But perhaps that was it. No one complained. Even at the best of jobs, before I slipped into this invisibility, there was always time for a good bitch and moan. It was conversational lubricant. It sped the clock hands, and if there was anything we needed, it was that. Not that we knew what was on the other side of time.

It was E. that cracked first. "I think Y. was lucky," he said aloud but to no one in particular. I was closest, watching grown men in shorts chase a ball in front of thousands on the television. "At least he knows he's dead." E. was a peculiar shape for our group. He was five-seven, spectacled, almost chubby. Average in every way, except for the Bermuda triangle of his hairline, which seemed to capture all the hair from his head into a neat geometric shape on top of his skull. But what truly set E. apart was the bastard was simply better than all of us. Faster. Craftier, more fearless. He never failed to complete The Run first. Even when snakes kept the east gate guarded, he used them like slithering stepping-stones and cut his journey in half. He'd clearly been an all-star in college, perhaps a pro in pick a sport. Midthirties now, E. had the skills of a god in the body of a troll, and he didn't even feel the need to gloat. He was so good it denied mentioning.

He scooted closer, twisting his college ring like a roulette wheel with no lucky numbers. "Y., lucky," he said. I'd earned my reputation for reticence since the punch and was in no mood to play therapist to another drunken purge. E. knew I wasn't a talker, but he still slid closer. "Don't kill me, kid," he said. "I'm just saying." I stood up. Turned off the TV, as if that shocking move would be the period to the night's sentence, and briskly walked toward the door. E.'s hand fisted around my bicep. He was as strong as he was skilled. To get release, it would have been a fight. "He was a good man."

"I'm sorry," I said. Surprised less by the words than by the fact that I meant them. E. let go and I stood there, as the blood chose shoulder or elbow in its returning flow.

"We shouldn't be here," he said. We? He and I? Or all of us. "We should go." His tone was flat as a postal clerk asking,

"Which stamps?" His eyes focused on the liquor bottles, their labels all peeled, making the liquid look fake. Then he rose, slid by me with a dancer's grace, went to his room, and put a rubber bullet in his head. We were now ten. This time, they sent a replacement.

Mc. was Irish the way rain is wet. His hair was the color of scorched clay, and he couldn't form a sentence without multiple pillars of "fuck." He was younger than I was, that was new. But his adoration for whatever the hell it was we were doing made it seem that he'd invented the place. Within a half hour he had spoken more than any of us had in months. Dirty jokes, lies, and a hilarious confessional stream to our group of heathen priests. Mc. told about the history of his family. His one-eyed aunt. His three-legged dog. His sister's boil with eyes like a potato. Everyone he knew had something wrong with them. Nephew hadn't spoken since they tied the bag over his head. Neighbor had cancer of the knee and fell into a well and drowned. Sister-in-law slept with both him and his brother before deciding who got the bride. Mc. was thrilled. He thought she was a lousy lay. "Me poor brother. Forty years of that bag of wet leaves." It wasn't that his stories were believable. In fact, in a place where we'd grown accustomed to mythologizing our autobiographies (training, we kidded ourselves, for undercover futures . . . Ego, it was: boys lie in locker

rooms; men lie in bars). Nor were they that funny or in-
structive. He was a muddler of punch lines and a saboteur
of sentiment. Rather, it was the sheer avalanche of them
that caught us in the end. The stadiums full of souls he
claimed to know. The line of women who had sampled his
wares. The cruel bosses, odorific teachers, maimed school
buddies, and thalidomidic twins. It was as if he'd eaten a
year's worth of local newspapers and vomited out the head-
lines.

They put Mc. in E.'s old room, two doors down from
me, and I could hear him pace at night. He had chronic in-
somnia, as did Thomas Edison, Napoleon, and Winston
Churchill, he'd been quick to inform me.

"Napoleon lost," I said.

"Two out of three."

"Two out of four."

"I haven't lost yet." He grinned, his teeth like badly
parked cars.

"You're here," I said. "Aren't you? That's got to constitute
some sort of failure." It was the most I'd spoken since my
first week at the hotel. Back when I still thought it was a
party, a prank, not a slow slide into identity removal. I knew
that we had to check our names at the door. But I'd never
liked mine very much, didn't think I'd miss it. Yet since E.'s
squeeze play got him home, I'd been dreaming of my mother

calling from the bottom of the stairs. And in the dream I was crying because, although there were steps in front of me, there seemed no way down. Dreaming about my mother frightened me. Men like us were supposed to be untethered, emotion-free, save for the exhilaration of violence and humiliation. Nightmares about mama and pajamas were not good armor for the psyche. I needed to butch up. I asked R. to increase The Runs.

Silence was his response, his expressionless face still latticed with wrinkles.

"How old are you, sir?" I asked. It was the first personal question I'd dared his way. R. shook his head, backed away like a gate-shy pony.

"This newbie's got us all fucked up." So R. was feeling it, too. Mc. had arrived with something viral. A personality. Verve. Life. That was it. And to a squad full of death specialists who weren't allowed to kill or die yet, life smelled like perfume. Or poison, if you were R. He couldn't afford to have his men looking forward to a night of Mc. bluster. He needed us dazed and inarticulate. Confused by the sun's place in the sky. The presence of Mc. had given order to our days. We were eating at the same time, whatever time it was, but together. People didn't want to hear a story secondhand. They wanted Mc.'s *ayems* and *huzzahs*. His stuttering innuendos and laughless jokes. Mc. had stepped into our blackness and not been absorbed.

R. decided to mess up the mojo. I'd wanted more of The Run? I got it. Three a day. Lights-out started immediately after the nightly recorded sports event. Then the TV disappeared. Even the booze was removed, leaving just beer and salad-dressing wine. But amid all the unfriendly changes, there had to be a break. An interim. A pause. And into that space bloomed Mc., our gospel proclaimer, our foul-mouthed fornicator. Our carnival barker with the megaphone voice and bright brown eyes. I began to worry that R. might kill him to restore order to the wolf pack. Sacrifice one for the survival of the unit. I found myself standing between R. and Mc. whenever we were in the same room, his subconscious shield, his bulletproof chest.

I tried to bring up the topic with a few of the others so I'd have backup if R. went for the target. I knew my cohorts needed Mc. as much as I did. L. used to laugh so hard at his jokes that he hissed like a leaking tire being chewed by a dog. But each time I broached the topic I was met with incomprehension. Though this lie was among their weakest, they were able to pretend I was crazy. That Mc. was no different from any of us. That things hadn't changed at all.

"You getting faggoty on us, kid?"

"Some of Velva's Aqua splash onto you when you garaged his larynx?" The men often reminded me of the killing, either to tell me that they weren't afraid or themselves that they were.

"So we're all alone, that's it?" I offered. "Hard world. Hard men."

"Live or die trying, bleeder."

"I stopped bleeding," I said.

"Looks like you started again."

Funny thing was, I had it wrong. R. didn't have a bullet for Mc. He had a promotion. After only ten spins inside, Mc. was given the first assignment any of us had had on the other side of the wall.

R. gave him his instructions, and Mc. left at dawn, turning around to popgun me from the door. "Genius never sleeps," he smiled, and light from the street I'd never seen sucked his thinness into its thinness and they both disappeared.

When I was a teenager, I used to paint in the room above our garage. The fumes of the cadmiums and ceruleans made me high enough to think I was good. I'd never find out. I burned all my paintings in the backyard after my brother stepped off a curb in town without looking. They said he had actually become a part of the driver, the impact was so great. They couldn't tell where some fifty-three-year-old man began and my twelve-year-old brother ended. Strangers become entwined in the oddest places. The death scene of an accident. Or a soldiers' hotel.

Because here I was, missing Mc. And remembering a question I had back when I was seventeen. What is the color of grape? I'd been trying every combination of blue and white, add pink, more white, pthalo blue, alizarin red, to get the color of grape juice. And after three weeks of exhausting my paint supply, I'd never even gotten close. I was going to ask my brother that afternoon. He was five years younger than I but already far smarter. And I remember berating myself for not asking him sooner. He would have mixed it for me with this ruler he always carried. To squash bugs, or scratch his back, or occasionally actually measure something. He would make grape with his ruler and the world would return to its place in the galaxy.

The ruler didn't break in the crash. It was the only thing.

Now here I was, waiting for Mc. to return from his assignment. As were the others, even R., though they hid their desire like boys at a middle-school dance. I had suddenly lost all interest in what story he had stolen from the outside world. I simply needed to ask him the color of grape.

Two days. Three. Seven. It didn't matter now that we were counting. R. had put a calendar grid without months or a year where the TV had been, and L. checked it off every morning that Mc. hadn't returned. R. cut back on The Run. We only had two during the days we didn't hear from Mc., and they were lazy affairs. The hunt and escape playing out on fading batteries. Once R. even rose up high enough to show his face from behind the blind. No one bothered to notice.

Like all things overly anticipated, the end came without fanfare or clarity. In the middle of the night, Mc. knocked on my door. My first instinct when I opened it was to gloat. He had come to tell me first. I was so focused on my worthiness, it took me a moment to see the haze over his eyes, like steam above a kettle. "Can't sleep," he said, his voice cracking.

"That's OK," I encouraged. "Geniuses."

"They don't need geniuses out there."

"We need them here," I said gently, as if to my brother. As if in my forsaken youth. And then I began to ask him, "What is the color of — ?" when Mc., useless as a broken ruler, collapsed into my arms.

We kept him in the dining room. There was a so-called infirmary, the old staff dressing area, where the waiters of this once glamorous hotel did their presto chango from wise-ass locals to continental servers. It was a cold, gray room with a halogen overhead that spooked on and off, its own Morse. Supplies consisted of refrigerated bags of everyone's blood types. Gauze. Coagulants. Iodine. Ibuprofen. Levaquin and penicillin. Not comprehensive armor against a war.

Mc. deserved the dining room. R. had us lug his bed and nightstand in, not easy with a king-size and its headboard. Even strong as we were, making the corners, taking the stairs made for a crude, scraping ballet. Mc. was conscious enough to thank us with a nod, a mumble, but not enough to mock us for our overconcern. Which is what the healthy Mc. would have done. He'd have collected ways to humiliate us for years to come if he'd seen us lend this much attention to any of our crew. But his mind had become a Nebraska road and he had no markers to help him keep track.

We all sensed that even the best hospital couldn't mend what was broken in Mc. It wasn't what had happened to him. It was something his own hands had done. The only sign of his mission was that the last three fingers on his left hand were burned and blistered over. His hair smelled of cordite and sulfur, so we guessed it was a bomb, and R.'s silence at our questions confirmed it. Mc. had been sent out to blow something up and in so doing had destroyed something fragile inside of himself.

When we'd signed up, we knew that there was a war. When two enemies had memorized the math of their hate, we would be sent in to alter the equation. One and one stops equaling two and starts equaling blood. This was included in the recruiting chat I was given while sitting at the far end of my local bar, reading a magazine someone had left behind.

The recruiter had used it as a conversation starter. Great article on disarmament on page seventy-two. I'd just been looking at the pictures, but this man, with his golfer's tan and candied breath, knew things about me like Jesus did in

the Bible. Not that I believed in Christ or anything close.
Not believing was part of my profile. One of the things that
got me noticed in the first place. They didn't want true believers. True believers had passion and direction. They didn't
yield to instruction. They were not human Play-Doh, ready
to be palmed and knuckled into the shape of the day.

No, they sought out guys exactly like me. Orphans, or
one-parenters. (My father had died of cigarettes and cyni-
cism when I was a teenager. His death had felt like a reprieve
from the governor. I remain grateful to Phillip Morris and
all their fine tobacco products.) Athletes that played well in
high school but never tried in college. Overachievers and
hard workers were anathema. Jail time. Preferably less than
a year, preferably for sudden violence. I was on probation at
the time of my visitation for taking a chair to a table full of
English tourists. All men, they had been laughing like thugs
too close to my quiet zone and dared to reject my request
for silence. Only reason I'd gotten probation was that one of
the victims was too tied up at work to travel back to the
States to attend the trial.

Ability to hold liquor. Apparently, one of the newest in-
terrogation techniques of the enemy was to loosen the
tongue of the captured through the generous proliferation
of rum and other spirits. I was told that they once watched
me drink eight whiskeys, six beers, and an ouzo, then drive

home and (this was their favorite part) parallel park in one move.

Disenfranchisement. A collective disappointment with everyone and everything, including oneself, was the clincher. The other skills could be taught. True disillusionment was a gift. My recruiter scooted closer when he told me that. Put his hand on my shoulder like a confidant or coach. "I want to hit you now," I had said, smiling. "Really fucking hard."

"Good," he smiled, his mentholated aroma sneaking out even through his gritted, frightened teeth. "But don't. Your country's already proud." He then slid me a napkin with a number on it. "That's per month." And the same smile, still hoping I wasn't going to earn his dentist a hefty fee as well.

I looked at the number for longer than I wanted to, unwilling to let him know how shocked and appreciative I was. "Have to work on your poker face, bleeder," he said. He walked out, leaving a hundred on the bar for the tab, the show-off. Then I really wanted to hurt him.

Even though he didn't mention a second meeting, I knew I'd only need to wait. And it suddenly dawned on me that whenever he or someone else did come for my answer, it wouldn't be only the second time. The man in line at the grocery store. His beard thick and dark-golden as a hive of bees. He'd chatted with me for five full minutes, with the express lane open and only two cans of coffee in his basket. We'd talked college football, showcasing our opinions like museum pieces for the clerk and other customers to admire. He asked me statistics, and I answered with the confidence and sudden steadiness of a ticker tape. He unspooled useless knowledge from me that I had no idea was woven inside my head. Made me feel uselessly smart. I thought, I like that guy, and even yelled, "Go Wildcats," to him as our cars passed in the parking lot, he in a convertible the color of a bullet.

The elderly gentleman at the post office who had asked for help sealing his envelope. "Arthritis," he'd said, "is a motherfucker." And I laughed, and he spoke of other frustrations in life. Politics. Marriage. Fathers. This had been another test. His envelope was addressed to the next town over, but the zip was wrong. When I corrected it for him, he thanked me and said, "Glaucoma is —"

"A motherfucker," I finished.

"I was going to say son of a bitch. But close enough." Thinking back, were his age spots real? Was that a thin sheen of glue around the hairline? Clearly I had been passing these tests.

Just before I went to pay with the golfer's hundred, I lifted it to the light. Looked OK, but I was no expert. I signaled the bartender and slid him the bill. "Do me a favor," I said, recognizing that he was new. "Sorry, I don't know your name."

"No, you don't," he said. "Yes, it's counterfeit. Keep it up, bleeder, you're scoring like a champ." He snatched the bill. I looked up. The place was empty. By the time I made it to the door, all the lights were off. My father would have liked that trick. He loved to posit that the world was run entirely behind closed doors yet equally in plain sight. No one was worthy of trust. He'd treated me as if I were a plant in his wife's womb. Maybe the bastard had been on to something.

Curiosity and fear are a dangerous cocktail. What draws you repulses you, and halfway through the journey you forget why you dared begin it, or how to get back. I'd joined up because I liked that I didn't know exactly what I was joining. I knew it was government work. I liked the paycheck and the anonymity. I liked that they thought they were smarter than me, while at the same time thought I was pretty damn smart. The night of the "intake" — their word — I had planned on bragging about all the details I'd caught. The old man's wig and zip code. The coffee cans and convertible. The woman at the diner who sat in the opposite booth and spoke Italian into her cell phone. And then French. And then English. Repeating the same piece of news in all three languages, something about a pair of shoes and an uncle in from out of town. When she left, she bumped my table and said, "*Pardonnez-moi*."

"*Pas grave*." I'd smiled. Then the same in Italian.

"You speak . . ." Almost flirting.

"Every one you just spoke except English." My mother listened to language tapes the way some women knit. Not that she was ever going anywhere. "Don't need a passport to learn," she'd say. Then repeat in French, German, etc. "I hope your uncle likes his shoes," I'd told the woman, toasting her with my empty water glass.

"I speak too loud." Embarrassment staining her perfect, pale face.

"Everyone does. Eventually all we'll have is yelling and email." She was pretty, and I wanted her to be just an attractive trilinguist with a hankering for diner pie. But by that point it was all too clear. She stepped close so that her skirt was pinned against my table and I could see the separation of her legs through the fine material. I flash-hoped that an evening with her would be my final test.

"Train station, *ce soir*, nine p.m. Don't pack." Before my witty rejoinder was fashioned into Italian, she was out the door, a handful of mints her final theft.

But there would be no bragging. That night two strangers, stronger than I, said hello and guided me down the platform steps. Three cars were waiting. We all got into the middle one. The first strongman manually opened my jaw. The other threw in a pill. "Chew," they both said. I spit it out. The second time they weren't so nice. Suffice it to say, I chewed, or they scissored my mouth with their hands to simulate chewing. And then I was drowsy. And then I was inside.

My hotel room was ornate, with blue couches decorated in gold like a captain's jacket, and a bed bigger than a man needs. The hangover from the knockout pill was not nearly as painful as the hangover from the knockout elbow to my ribs that had preceded the chewing of said pill. Sitting up was like peeling a magnet off a fridge. Except I felt like the magnet *and* the fridge. When I did get to my feet, I was still dressed, shoes included, and a bottle of whiskey was my reward. Showered in the enormous double shower. Shaved with a hotel razor and cream. I put on the robe, since the entire thing felt like pretending. Let the terrycloth soak up the water and padded around my suite like a businessman waiting for a hooker.

First sign of trouble: the TV didn't work. And at these prices, I laughed to myself. Next sign: the clothes I'd just slipped out of were gone. Replaced by . . . all my clothes. The closet was now stocked with everything from my closet at home. The shirts and one suit were hanging. The pants, socks, boxers, junior-college sweatshirt all folded and drawered. Sneakers, shoes, belts, turtlenecks. Every stitch of fabric I owned (there wasn't much) and a few I'd forgotten about were now housed in my new dwelling place. I got dressed over my still partially wet skin, careful to keep my back to any imagined cameras. R. would chuckle at me days later about how I assed the cameras every chance I got. He didn't know I wasn't mooning, I was trying to hide.

With a moth-nibbled sweater and frayed jeans on, I went to the curtains to see where I'd agreed to come. They didn't open. They'd been adhered to the wall. And behind the curtain I could feel the thick chill of corrugated metal. I imagined that hadn't been standard in all suites on the hotel's opening night. And no amount of yanking or tearing yielded anything but a rash on my hands. So this was the deal. Beautiful room. No view. Ever.

The first few nights, no one visited. I guessed they were nights. It didn't matter. I figured that the solitary confinement — my door locked from the outside, no access or egress through the vents or ceiling (I checked) — was part of the disorientation program. The first experiment of malleability. And since I'd agreed to take this magicless mystery tour, and since I couldn't figure a way out of the damn room, I decided to be as malleable as possible. I lounged around. I napped. I ate what they placed in my room. (Always and only after I had drifted off to sleep.) And I swigged the whiskey. Outside, in the distance, there was a staccato of bombings. Like a child practicing drums poorly to annoy his teacher. Some fell from the sky. Others threw their nails and fire out from the street. Skybombs sounded like a diver from a height. Street-sides sounded like my brother being hit by that car. Over and over again. I stopped remembering it and simply started living it. His death became present to me. And that was when I stopped being afraid.

Until Mc. Until he lay there, his face as bloodless as the moon, and looked up at us with something terrible and important to say. But his lips bounced off each other like two trampolines, crushing the words in between.

If Mc. had been able to tell us, the terror would have lifted. He could have spun one of his stories, even if it included unspeakable horrors, and we still would have fallen to hysterics. His tales were alchemical, pain into gold, and we were men in need of gold. But his silence, his defeat at the hands of life outside the hotel, sowed in each of us a darkness that bloomed by the hour. Our minds had become furrowed with fear, and roots had grown so deep, we were immobilized.

R. knew we would cease to be a unit if the weather didn't break. We needed a change of subject. And that could only come with the removal of our obsession. The dining room was sealed, save for the single entrance from the kitchen. Mc., and the fear he was contagious with, was quarantined. Only L. and R. were allowed to visit, to check his vitals, administer his meds. L. was our only physician and was, at that time, the only reason Mc. was still alive.

They let us say our good-byes, most of which consisted of a punch on the arm or a tousle of the hair. Mc. was asleep during much of the ritual but awoke briefly when I knelt low to tell him something. "It's OK if you don't wake up," I whispered. "It's all right to sleep." He turned his head as I rose, as if to scratch his ear from a secret wind.

"No," he said, still looking sideways. "You know I can't sleep." A half smile was all he managed after this, his first full sentence since his collapse. I looked around to see if I had a witness, but L. was busy counting out pills in the far corner.

"You son of a bitch," I whispered. "Are you faking?" The haze rose again across his eyes, his mouth pulled dry. If he was faking, he was Houdini reborn. L. chased me out before I could get any more. And that was the last I saw of Mc. for a while. Because R. had a second tier to his plan to shake our lethargy. He would send another soldier out on a mission. A soldier who would return emboldened, electric, vigorous with the violence he had seen and caused. And that soldier would be me.

I was married once, when I was twenty. It had been three years since my brother's death, and I woke up one April morning and realized I was sick of being sad. It was a strange day to have such a revelation. It was raining so hard by ten a.m. that the streets were flooded, garbage and toys flowing through the gutters. My mother was at work, my father now dead long enough for the house to feel nearly

free of his ghost. Nearly. I tiptoed downstairs like a boy afraid
to startle Santa, had a bowl of Rice Krispies avalanched in
sugar, and stepped into the soak of it all for a good old-
fashioned walk in the rain. It was about two and a half miles
from our house to the center of our little village, and by the
time I'd finished sluicing across lawns and hydroplaning over
the copless streets, I was a single, giant molecule of water as
I stepped into the ice cream parlor with the famous name.
The bell rang at my entrance, and a girl looked up from behind that angled glass counter. She'd been losing a wrestling
match with a bucket of Rocky Road, her face rosy with refrigerated frustration. "Don't open till eleven-thirty."

"I'll wait," I said. "Funny time, though." She returned to
her battle without answering. I suppose I didn't look like
much of a catch, my clothes and hair all pasted to my then-
skinny frame. "Not eleven, not noon. Funny."

"Superstition." She grunted from behind the glass. "My
boss is weird. Can you help me with this?" My rain hands
froze to the carton as I wrestled it free. I presented it to her
like a doctor handing over a newborn. Her eyes said a long
thank-you.

"Take it," I said. "It hurts."

They opened at 11:30 and closed at 9:15, thanks to
weirdo boss, so I had nine hours and forty-five minutes to
kill awaiting our first date. That was time enough to go
home, shower, change, change again, change again. Shower

off the sweat I'd accumulated from changing so many times and then go shopping for some new clothes. I was so caught off guard by this adrenaline rush of happiness that I never stopped to question it. I thought, I don't remember this feeling, so I must not understand it enough to recognize it, so just let it rain. Which it was still doing when I left to pick her up. My mother squeezed my hand, as if she'd been alerted to my plans, encouraged by them. But I hadn't told her. There simply seemed to be things a mother did know.

It was 9:16, and she was standing outside the store, with an umbrella playing keyboard to the rain's mad fingering. It sounded better than Chopin. Her name was MK, and she was seventeen/eighteen, depending on when I asked her and what she thought I had in mind.

We went for pizza. I burned my tongue. Between soda refills, I fell in love. I hadn't kissed a girl since before the accident, so I was pretty sure I was getting it wrong, but she coached me through. In the front seat of my car, she turned up the radio and made me mute with pleasure. Six weeks later, we got our blood tests and Mom was our witness.

Things happen like this in small towns. Life moves at such sudden speed against the endless backdrop of previous slowness that a temporary blindness sets in. Like watching the landscape along the highway. We think we see houses. Or trees. Or signs. But they remain unnamed and unvisited. They are the blur that allows our actual lives to feel as if they have shape. But then the speed returns to normal. When we pull over and see that all that lies ahead is the same vast nothing that lies behind, a sadness sets in that no April rainstorm can trick upside down.

We lasted less than a year. I got mean or maudlin or forgetful enough to chase her and her first earned tears back to her parents' house. And back behind the frozen glass with the jimmied cones. I hadn't been made of the materials she deserved to sustain her. My joints and bolts would have given out on some more important date, like the birth of a child or a truly honest conversation about the one dream she really had. So that still feels like a favor, these years later. I pulled her away from the approaching train of my cruelty. My indifference. The weakness at the center of what constituted my heart.

But on that predawn morning when R. sent me out (with rain needling down), I felt something I had never experienced before. I missed my ex-wife. Missed the baby-powder smell of her too-long neck. The frayed end of her ponytail, the quiet of her sleep. Missed the word *wife* itself, and that I had ever been so foolish as to ex the word out. R. slammed the front door of the hotel behind me, the wood sounding certain and final, and for the very first time, I saw where I was.

Not that I could put a name to all the destruction. It was clear it was a city, or had been. There were miles of buildings in ruins, and even the billboards and street signs had long melted to rust. The skyline was crooked as a boxer's mouth, and the air was thick with the detritus of bombs. My mind rolodexed all the factors that make up a place. I inhaled for the possibility of the sea but garnered only a hacking cough against all the glass and fiberglass dancing in the air. Checked signage to gain the local language, but there wasn't a font to be found. Along with the hard matter this war had destroyed, it had also burned down every last word. I scanned the embered architecture for anything familiar, but all buildings look the same at two moments: before they are built and after they fall down.

I was exposed, just standing in front of the hotel, but exposed to what? I still hadn't been told who the enemy was, just that it existed and needed to be eradicated. Or irritated. Or instigated. But at the very least engaged. That was the term R. used as he filled my rucksack with the mission's supplies. "Engage the enemy," he'd said. Which had made me think of my ex. I'd never engaged her. I'd simply married her, skipping the on-ramp, going right for the highway. Perhaps if I'd engaged her, we might have had better luck. Too late for luck. I was outside my womb, breathing heavily for my life, and looking for the enemy without knowing where to look. Perhaps this is what had happened to Mc. He'd heard the door close behind him. Locked up with panic and stood precisely on this spot for thirteen days. What he'd returned to us with was not horror but shame. Humiliation. The cowardice of his soul. I checked the dust for footprints. The mark of Mc.'s mudwing boots. But no. His fingers had been burned. He'd lit a fuse or planted a detonator. He was guilty. That was the haze in his eyes.

I checked the straps on my rucksack, pinning it tight to my back like a nervous father hanging onto his child at a ball game. Because inside was everything I had been told that I'd need to survive. If I went down, I was going to be buried with all the necessary supplies in my patrol pack: Seven shirts. Seven underwear. Seven pairs of socks. Thirty days worth of MREs with heater to cook the hot dogs and heat the cocoa, and Tabasco to kill the taste. Toothpaste, brush, soap, shaving cream, and razor. (A clean shave lets the gas mask seal onto the face.) 550 cord, Gerber tool, batteries, chem lights, gas mask, and flashlight. All that was for staying alive. Then there were the weapons to make sure the other guy stayed deader than me. M4 carbine with scope. Bayonet. Seven Mag load (two hundred twenty bullets). Two grenades. One smoke grenade. And another six mags in a bag. Phosphorous grenade to light a truck up like a fireplace on wheels. Stun grenades (flash-bang) to get at least ten seconds of enemy incapacitation from the concussion boom.

Like Mc., I'd been sent out without a radio. R. had said all satellite feeds were down, and any iterant noise in the field could make us a sudden target. Even a zeroed-out tac-com was deemed too risky. Our job was to survive and engage alone. Army of one indeed.

My ballistic helmet and SAPI vest, with its front and back plates made of bulletproof porcelain, only served to make my legs feel more vulnerable. I tucked my boot knife into my boot's shallow, close to the grab. And held my Beretta, with its three fifteen-round magazines, plus backup, just to make sure it was there.

Three hundred ten bullets. Two guns, two knives, a couple of grenades and just enough protection to make me feel unsafe. I was a walking ammo store. An Ohio Blue Tip match waiting for its tip to be scratched. I wanted to go inside. I wanted to go . . . not home, but away. And I knew I couldn't do either.

The Run, I thought. Motion is salvation. Figure out all the details later, after I'm still alive. Right now, lift your lactic-acid-heavy legs, bow your head, run, and crouch, like you've seen in the movies. Talk to yourself in the second person like a lunatic, but move, move, move!

The sun rose as I scrambled, but it made little difference. All the vague ocher outline gave me was which way was east. I counted my steps to guarantee backtrack to the hotel, in case of darkness or failure or, shit, it didn't matter. I wasn't sent out to come back. Not until I had engaged. And that would mean getting lost to do it. "Ninety-four, ninety-five." I promised myself I'd stop counting at one hundred.

"One-o-one, one-o-two." The faster I ran, the louder my feet sounded, and I felt certain I was announcing my arrival like a father back from work. "One-thirty-four, one-thirty-fuck —" I went down hard. My rucksack fumbled forward, and I scrambled to recover it, aware of its contents and their necessity in case of engagement.

I didn't see what I'd tripped on until after I circled back. A human arm. It wasn't severed, just the only thing jutting clear from the collapsed structure that crushed the life from this . . . person. Time had robbed the arm of sexual identifiers and most of its skin. The bone shone through like white metal in the early light. I crossed myself like a dilettante and hurried on. I took shelter behind the closest thing I could find to a standing wall. It consisted of drywall and a tangle of wire, with a hole in it the size of a bear. It seemed to be part of a basement that had been blown all the way up to the surface. Next to me were three perfect rungs from a ladder, but without any of their partners. A furnace thermostat had been set to seventy-two degrees when it melted from another heat, and leaning on that was a ping-pong paddle, its rubber seared clean. Just above where the handle fit into the hand of the player who'd been playing. An interrupted game that would not begin again.

Was I so unhappy that I chose this? I thought, my shirt now wrapped around my face to filter the spangled air. Or did this choose me? I could've said no. Yet I'd gone to the train station. I'd abandoned my shabby life. Boredom: that was the skill they didn't mention. But all of us excelled at it. We were bored enough to opt for this unknowing, and we could adjust to boredom well enough to sit inside the hotel until the tumblers spun our way. The fact was, we didn't want action. We'd spent our lives being passive while hallucinating we were doers. Our complaints and opinions convinced us we were in the idiot world but not of it. The reality was, the twelve of us had subsisted primarily on inertia. Our barstool brawls and fisted threats proved only our self-hatred and our fear. To be silent, as I was that morning, to be on a mission with a purpose, however vague, was precisely what none of us knew how to do. It was why we survived The Run. That was a mile in a maze. A guaranteed finish, even if it was a bullet bruise that never healed. The unmapped expanse I was presently tripping across was what lurked at the very border of our panic. That was why I kept running and counting. Stopping would mean needing a plan. Mc. had come outside and found out that all he was was stories. He didn't want to live them, just tell them. And that was what had shut him up. He was back there dying from the lack of himself. And I was out here finding out if I knew how to live.

It took a land mine to begin the answer to the question. It went off late. The gravel shifted under my feet, and I knew as I pushed off what was next. But the mechanism had rusted, or the mine was from another battle, forgotten by the dust. In that pause just before "Yes, my leg is gone," I realized I wanted my leg. Desired it. Even loved it. I thanked it for all it had run me over, past, and through. I had a sense of its solidity for the very first time, just before the shrapnel spiked up through the skin. It was solid all right, but the AP frag's artillery was solider, and the pain pierced through like ecstasy until my face wept with sweat and my pant leg blossomed from the inside out. There was also blood down my slit cheek, and my chest, just above the vest, grew warm with a gentle spill, but my leg had caught the pass. I scrambled back, sightless as a crab in all the murk.

I didn't hear the sniper fire yet. I was too busy praising my leg for still being attached to my body. I took shelter between two windowless cars, their frames big enough to carry a family I hoped hadn't been inside. I tore open my pant leg the rest of the way and saw the metal sticking two inches straight out of my calf. Blood bubbled out like a tub emptying in reverse. Then the bullets pinging against charred metal, sparking flecks and shards across my torso like tiny snowflakes. My land mine had rung the doorbell, and somebody was definitely home.

More bullets, more misses, and I didn't move. I knew that the sniper would never leave his perch, for that is his only power. A shooter is often weakest up close, so the threat of him tiptoeing in to finish me was almost nil. I had time to work up the courage to yank this shank out of my leg. I just started laughing. Was it recalling a joke about the Irish and their twins that Mc. told poorly every time he got tipsy? Was it the memory of my father slipping on the driveway after cursing the winter for sending snow? Whatever the trigger, I laughed harder and louder than I had since a child. The louder I laughed, the faster the bullets came, the ruined autos like an orchestra of ammunition. Some bullets got even closer, sending rubble hard across my face, and on I laughed. It felt as if I hadn't breathed in years, and the polluted molecules entering my lungs felt like diamonds of light.

Laugh. That's it. Keep laughing. Louder. Bullets. Louder. Closer. Louder. Louder. Rip. Out came the shank in one glorious pull. The hole in my leg showed how close I had come to having my tibia sawn in two. But the wound was clean and the architecture of my arteries looked scraped but sound. I used strands of pant leg to tourniquet the leg, and the bleeding quickly slowed. My rucksack contained a cauterizer, which I poured into the hole like sugar into coffee. My head fluttered with the pain, as if I had tumbled from a height, then calmed as the flow was stemmed. I breathed. Laughed one last time, and then, without warning or desire, I fell fast asleep.

In my dream there was chatter. Like a conversation of birds. Or a language learning itself as it was spoken. I'd been told as a teenager that everyone in a dream was you. But there was no one in this dream. So was I the sound? The trickle and bang? The slipstream solace. The underlying hum. The landscape was water, made solid as glass. Whispers and wind glanced off the clear surface of things. Every moment was a rumor. Every rumor was true.

Like a cloud, I floated above, but not in the sky. The sky was woeful and lonesome, stars like injuries across its pained black skin. There came the warble of being followed. Anger disguised as music, catching up to wherever all my nothing was. From the side of the air popped moles of light. Oval and perfect as popsicles in summer. The music grew louder and longer, stretching itself to trick me from in front. Without eyes, I saw it all, from my dangling perch between above and below. I was afraid. I was fearless. The bass thump of my heart fluttered and panicked like a cat in a bag. Where should I look when there was nothing I wanted to find?

I woke up with a gun to my lips. "I was dreaming," I said to my enemy, as if he were my mother come to rouse me for school. He didn't speak. His only communication was the slightest tremble in his hands. It was his fear that he was trying to communicate, trying to transpose his virus onto mine. This was my sniper, up close. He had mistaken my sleep for death and had come to take whatever was left of me. Supplies. Clothing. He didn't expect to find me alive. And now, face-to-face with another human, he was unable to erase my face. The gun tasted bright blue in my mouth, and the air was so mottled with backflash that I could only make out his eyes. They were whiteless slits squinting against the smog. The rest of his face was smeared with dirt and camo, making him green/black as a nature-show subject. The only sign that he was a man was the cactus poke of whiskers through his cake of filth. It wasn't a thick growth, so he'd either been in safety until recently, or he had the sparse beard of an Asian man or a young boy. He stood and trembled. I remained in repose, unable to mount a defense or even lift my hands in surrender. We were frozen as garden sculptures waiting for the rich to pass us by. My life did not flash before my eyes. But his did.

I saw him running with a kite up a sun-whipped beach where the stones and shells had turned the color of Easter eggs. I saw him kissing a girl on a swing that ached with summer rust, the chain as dark red as his lover's lips. I saw him pack a suitcase, board a train, wave at strangers, whistle an unwritten tune. I saw him purchase gloves and lose them. Steal a Seckel pear from a tree, not to eat, but to throw. Ride an escalator backward to make his sister laugh. I watched him climb a tree to flee a dog, only to find a cat on a limb.

When he reached to rescue, it slit his skin like tissue paper. I discovered him playing the autoharp for a collection of elderly women, his hands delicate over monotonous hymns. There he went, swimming in shoes to make his arms stronger and darning a sock because he'd learned how, and what was the use of knowing something and never doing it.

Then on a sled, avoiding trees as if protected, until a low-limbed fir split his lip into two separate lands interrupted by a lake of blood. He caught a fish with his hands like a grizzly. He unwrapped birthday presents as if they'd disappear if he didn't beat the clock. That was him at the parade, afraid amid the knees and thighs, glimpsing daylight and floats through a pinhole of limbs. He finished third at the track meet, slipped at the market, fell on his knees on Christmas morn. Then, at last, he was loading a rifle, his hands slick with sweat and oil. Hiding behind the ribs of a building, aiming at movement like he could win a prize. I even saw him walking down the rubble staircase to loot my remains. And when he saw me. The gentle lift of my chest. The slackjawed dreaming. The truth of my vividity. My self.

It had taken him a long while to lift the gun to my mouth. Tears had cut jagged lines into his mask of dirt. And it was then that I realized he had never put his finger on the trigger. "Do you speak English?" I barely spoke. No answer. He suddenly seemed to be looking past me. The rifle tip pressed hard into my lips so that my teeth leaned back in preparation. "Can you tell me," I managed, "where we are?" He lowered the gun. It drifted down my chin, across my chest, groin, legs, and then away. I wanted to say thank you. For showing me his life instead of mine. For not having the nerve to end me. But my mouth became dry as old bread, and my throat sealed itself against the effort of words.

He backed away at first, his eyes remaining on what was behind me. It didn't appear to frighten him. Through the veil of grime, one reaction was evident. Surprise. After twenty blind steps, his feet not bothering to test for solid ground, he fell. On his ass, free and boneless as a child. Did he laugh? Or give up? When he rose he turned his back to me and began to walk farther into the open passageway I had taken to reach this hiding place. His body passed in and out of view through the flickered light. "Hallelujah," he said, though he seemed too far away for me to hear, and it had come to my ears unshouted. Then, into a patch of clear again.

"Thank you," I finally said, and he turned back in time to watch the bullet enter his chest. I looked to see if I was holding a gun. He dropped to his knees, his strings cut, and pantomimed his death with dark grace. I held no gun, and felt forgiven. Then I crawled to my knees, coiled like a sprinter, and ran into the bulletproof air. He had taken my number in the checkout line. Today, I thought, I do not have to wait to die.

The first time I can remember getting into serious trouble was when I burned my little brother with hot chocolate. We were nine and four, walking through an out-door zoo, the day as hard and mean as a blade. Our parents had drifted to warmer environs. My mother stood in the gift shop, looking at her reflection and the postcard rack, back and forth. My father stood at the edge of the lizard tanks, looking like a cousin, wrinkled and lethal, his tongue dart-ing out to be rid of tobacco leaves.

My brother and I had been given hot chocolate to keep our gloveless hands warm, then pushed toward the polar bear exhibit as if we were bait. I kept tabs on my brother by listening for the shuffle of his boots, and waited for the mushroom clouds of steam to subside from the hot choco-late. But they refused. Apparently, our beverages had been heated by Satan, and any hope of actually drinking them had to be deferred until our college years. We found a bench across from the polars, for whom the day also seemed an in-sult. They hid in their caves and breathed plumes of smoke to rival our hot chocolates'. We seemed to be communicat-ing like Indians across the expanse. And all of us were saying, "It's fucking cold."

But not the hot chocolate. It refused the cold, dared it. Absorbed it without yielding. My brother and I found out when he pulled on my sleeve, inviting the chocolate in a cascade across his little legs. His thin corduroys were like paper towels, pulling the liquid through without delay. And my sweet little brother screamed so loud, all the animals went silent. All except my father, who slithered fast as a Komodo across the icy walk and lifted me with a fist that was both removal and a punch. My apology clotted just before it reached my throat. He left my screaming brother to my mother. She'd soothe while he satisfied his own anger by having a target and an excuse.

My brother's wounds took two weeks to heal. I pondered suing the hot chocolate maker, even called up the zoo in a disguised voice, calling myself a name I thought sounded scary. But the response was always the same. "It's the weird kid again."

Little brother apologized to me, aware that his tug on my sleeve had given me a double shiner and a wheezy cough from where Father squeezed my chest so hard. "It's not either of our faults," I explained. "It's the goddamn hot chocolate people. And they don't even care." We swore to never drink hot chocolate again. No hot beverage of any kind, in fact. Which would go on to cause us to covertly slip ice cubes in our soup at dinner for at least a year. Until we eventually simply forgot.

That's what I was thinking as I ran across the rubble and the road. All the things I had forgotten. They seemed to rush up at me from all sides, like traffic finally freed. I should have been concentrating on a place to dig in, or hide, or even a coward's sprint back to the hotel. But with every step another memory spidered up my spine. Sledding off our roof on snow days, landing on a ramp I'd built. Landing smooth and feeling the wind up my nostrils, the falling snow kissing my open eyes, adding to their whiteness. Another step and my brother's funeral, the casket surrounded by men in suits I did not know. They formed a circle strong as a cult, and I could not see what was left of him. My mother kept her back to the altar and helped seat people like a movie usher. There seemed the smell of popcorn in the air. But I needed to stop remembering. When I got to the end, I'd die like my enemy. I needed to have no past to erase if I wanted a future.

I looked up for the first time since I'd started running. The fog was just as unyielding as before, but it had bloomed brighter. The sun must have finally come out. I gazed skyward, eager to track direction and time like a good, frightened soldier. The light did not seem to be coming from above. But around. Just like the heat. I had run myself directly into the center of a fire. I couldn't discern what it was that was burning down around me, or if it was even a thing. The aromas of metal and flesh and oil had shaved into one sense. A sting. To breathe was pain, but it was not educational. The only way to find my way out of the flames was to walk more closely to them.

Heat bubbled my skin, taking fine hairs like a first crop.

The rubber of my boots blistered and adhered to my feet. I was glad to be alone, because if I had spoken, my face would have torn open at the seams from the heat. I was made of paper and twigs. My bones kindling, my flesh aching to be ash. OK, I thought, this is who I've become. A man unafraid of his own cremation. I walked and walked, my eyebrows curling into gone. My tongue warm. My thighs prickly as my brother's long-ago burns. One last step, I promised, and it won't hurt anymore. One. Last. Step. Instead, I fell laughing into the water. I laughed because even before I hit the liquid, I knew where I was. I caught a glimpse of the ruins of the fire escape. That's what made me laugh. Fire. Escape. Didn't know I was actually on fire until the water put me out. Then I decided to stay under. Like a baptism. Fire and water. As if I would surface brand-new. When, gasping, I did, the only new thing was the knowledge. The hotel was gone.

I put out the fire one bucket at a time. I used an ice bucket from the bar, kicking it into the pool to cool it, then dumping water on every maw of fire until the air was once again toothless and gray. Whatever had bombed us had dropped and deployed, and it was clear from what I found inside, the assault had come without warning.

B.'s torso sat at one end of the cafeteria, a fork still in his hand. His dinner and legs sat untouched on the steel table, its temper impervious to the flames. K. and L. were downstairs in the billiard room. The explosion had sealed them below, and both died with their mouths sucking for clean air from the bottom of the door. They were Siamese close, arms interlocked, faces black as burned chicken. I found the rest scattered about the hotel. Some too burned to identify save for the room or an unmelted ring. Others died with their hands over their ears, as if what they didn't hear wasn't happening.

I was able to dig enough holes in the rubble with the ice bucket to set all of the men at least a few feet below the hell they'd died in. It was the most I'd ever felt like a soldier, burying my platoon like God was watching and their families were, too. I was about to utter a wordless prayer when I finally did my math. One body was missing. Mc.'s.

I raced through the ruins like a game of hide-and-seek. Even was foolish enough to call out his name. But he was not there. First, a mad rush of relief. He was alive. They hadn't gotten him. I still had an ally, someone worth venturing back out to look for. Then, an elevator's descent of grief. He'd already died. He was sickly when I'd left, and hadn't made it through. He was already buried on the grounds. This was the saddest death of all.

I returned to the graves and feigned crossing myself. Whatever protection these men had needed had soured and expired. With the earth saturated with wet embers and a wind beginning to spin at my feet, I decided to stay the night. Or day. It didn't matter. Time had become as

meaningless as a stranger's face. The only part of the hotel
that hadn't been completely destroyed was the subbasement. Built with reinforced concrete and steel, it had survived the onslaught nearly unscathed. Even the stairwell
leading down was only dusted with debris. I snaked past
wires that dangled like nooses, around the generators and
heating system. The AC hub and electrical hot boxes. I had
never been this far down, and the air was remarkably clear.
My flashlight guided me to the janitor's supply closet, where
a mop and bucket uselessly stood guard.

Deeper still I wandered, my flashlight curious as an aard-
vark's nose. Doors hid nothing. R. had long ago emptied the
place of supplies for our use. Then to the farthest corner and
one last door. It had been glass, now shattered, and the
doorknob jimmied off. I eased in, suddenly afraid. I didn't
like pieces that didn't fit. A glass door among all this metal.
A missing doorknob. More chaos was not what I needed.
Even as I yearned to see this final corner of what had been
my home, I yearned more deeply to run away again. To be
dodging bullets and mines, fighting fires, talking snipers into
dying. I did not want this cramped office, shards of glass. This
alone.

The brand name was famous. I recognized it from a
thousand heist movies. The definition of excellence. The one
that no one could crack. Four feet by three feet of impene-
trability. But this safe was open. Not by a drill or dynamite

but by the combination. It was also full. Stack upon stack of dollars. And euros. And yen. And yuan. I'd been needing a clue about location, but all these notes gave me were impossible riches and nowhere to spend them.

I emptied the safe, counting the money out of boredom. I stopped when it went into millions and I wasn't a third of the way through. Then I reached into the dark back of the empty safe and knew why I'd been afraid. Into my hand fell three detonators. The flashpoint trigger mechanisms used to light plastic explosives. And behind them, a fresh batch of C-4, Semtex. The package was open, with just enough missing to make it clear. The goods R. had told us we'd be getting a shipment of. A shipment that had never arrived. He'd complained about it enough to make it true. I checked the box. No military markings. Just a box full of boom and no sender to return it to. As my shaking hands made a stuttering silhouette against the wall, I realized why Mc. wasn't upstairs among the dead. He hadn't come back to recuperate from some unseen horror. He had gone out to gather that which he was missing (hence the burns on his fingers, from handling raw chem), and he had come back playing broken to blow us all to hell.

Now I had an enemy. Now I had a war. And the beginning of my fury was aimed at me. How could I have fallen for the bluster and bravado? For his stammering address and his baseless confidence? Was I so in need of a hero that I chose a fool? Yes, he had added color to a bullet grayness that armored my days, but wasn't I smart enough to recognize that he'd come back a faker? A TV version of shell shock. The slack mouth. Dull eyes. And he'd even winked his good-bye to me, as if he'd gotten away with something before he'd even dared it.

Asshole. Dupe. Slave, I chastened myself while I gathered supplies for my exodus. My search-and-destroy mission. Anger gave me light. X-ray vision. I took the detonators, scattered meals from the melted kitchen (government food is built to survive the nuclear option), and enough water to keep me quenched until. Until what, I didn't know. I had no plan for my encounter with Mc. No particular map to guide me to him. I simply knew that having a target, and this sweet bile of revenge on the back of my tongue, had given me an energy I hadn't felt since the first Run. Or killing Y. Maybe I was truly good at killing. Created for it. Everything around me seemed to die, whether I wished it or hoped against it. Brother. Father. All my comrades at the hotel. Even the sniper who spared my life. I was contagious with death. And I felt like infecting Mc.

With my rucksack ready, I walked upstairs to where the door used to be, looked back one final time at the ruination, and memorized the mayhem. "Mc.," I actually spoke. "Here I come."

Can you have a destination if you don't know where you are going? And if you get there, is it luck, destiny, or the same fucking thing? I left the hotel thinking I had a target and within moments felt I was all target. Not to anonymous snipers anymore, or nefarious enemies TBD. But I pictured Mc., sitting on a pile of detritus, lighting a cigarette on the embers of a dead man's clothes, waiting for me to present close enough for a kill shot. So I walked serpentine, silly as a movie I'd laughed at as a kid. What was I doing out here? Why wasn't I stuck in the dead-end job, swapping gossip with po-faced coworkers? Why wasn't I lamenting gas prices and the mortgage crisis? Where were my wife, toys in yard, broken Jacuzzi, ants down the hallway wall? Back home I had felt nothing, but to trade it for this . . . something emptier than nothing. Existence without markers. Highway without exits. Fear without meaning. That was it. I was afraid, but my fear was untethered. I wasn't afraid to die but scared nonetheless. Perhaps I was already dead, and this was the dreadful unwinding of eternity. Hell wasn't other people. Hell was yourself, forever, waiting to encounter other people who wanted you dead. War isn't hell, I realized. Hell is war.

I was suddenly filled with a desperation to know where I was. I felt as though I would drown in the muddled air if I didn't find a road sign, an emblem, a detail that said this is here and not somewhere else. If I knew the city, even if I'd never been there, I figured I could bluff my way. This way's the river. This was the capitol building. Famous hospital. Local university. Playground donated by a man rich enough to have his memory bronzed. And then forgotten.

I slowed my rapid pace to snoop like a metal detector sniffing the sands of Miami Beach. I'd avoided this on my first sortie from the hotel because I didn't want to see limbs and heads as the only signposts. But burying pieces of my company had cured me of that. I began to look at everything as parts. The parts make the whole. The whole is made up of parts. Each is identifiable without the other. A finished building hides its ingredients. A single bolt holds within it the promise of its endgame. Look. No, don't look. See.

Archaeologists build careers out of shards of pottery. That was what I needed. Items of common use. A plate. A bowl. A Japanese temple. A hand-worn Hebrew bible. Chinese fortune sticks. A Russian doll.

"What are ya looking for?" The voice didn't startle me as much as it should have. I thought I was talking out loud to myself.

"Proof," I said.

"It's not here," the voice said. It was higher and happier than mine. I jerked up and put my hands in the air like the loser in a kung fu movie. "Nothing left here," it said. "You need to go further in." I tried to calculate if Mc. could pinch his voice into such a register. In the invisible light, anything seemed possible.

"Where are you?" I shouted, lowering my arms to feel my way.

The answer was a hand slipped into mine. It was a boy, maybe twelve. He was small, but his face was criss-crossed with enough scars to make it look like mended cloth. He spoke through lips that had only recently healed. "This way, then."

"I can't go with you," I spat, angry as a teacher, helpless as a student. "I am still looking."

"I can take you there." His eyes were purple. The color of grape.

"No," I said, meaning yes. Meaning please, meaning breathe for me. Anything but no.

"I've taken others," he said, and now we were walking. His pull was powerful, and his hand, though resting softly in my larger palm, was strong as a rudder.

"But I need to find a man. He killed . . ." I stopped, wanting to protect this ravaged man-child from any more disconnected tragedy.

"Everybody has killed." His voice like water over rocks. "I have killed. You have killed."

"How do you know?"

"Everyone knows," and I almost thought I heard him say my name. It was my adhered boots crushing a ceramic remain. A bowl, I thought, even as I let him lead me deeper into the murk. As I forgot to ask him our location.

"What is your name?" I said, suddenly unable to look at his map of scars.

"I," he said and fluttered a laugh out like an escaping dove in a magic trick. "It's a funny name, that's why . . ."

"Are you the last one . . . of your kind?"

"There are others," he said. I slowed down so I could take in more of him at an angle. He wore material more than clothing, and his feet were shod in tar. His hair was long and too filthy to be saved. Only if it were shaved would it yield its true color. His left ear, beneath the matted locks, was at least half missing.

"You can hear me?"

"The other one's extra good." Then we were walking faster. If my size hadn't allowed me to take one step to his three, I would have been running. Yet his gait looked unhurried to the eye. My lungs burned with sulfur and dust. I began to formulate a hundred questions to ask him, but asthma clouded my trachea and I traded words for breath. The more difficult it became to breathe, the easier it became to see. Up ahead, less than a football field away, the sun seemed to actually be the sun, and it was reflecting down on an area covered in foliage. Trees heavy with green leaves. A circle of flowering shrubs and plants. A veritable garden in the middle of all this death. I wanted to sprint toward it, press all the pure green against my face and feel its organic life. As we drew closer, I could see birds on potted plants. The orange of a bird of paradise, the white of a calla lily, a violet's own bright blue.

"We should run," I said. "Before . . ." But I was alone. My hand held no hand. The air behind me was thick as quicksand and it stole my eyesight. I called the boy's name once. Then didn't have the heart to say it again. Or to turn back around. There were no flowers and fruit trees on the horizon. Just more blowback and loss. The misery of the mirage hangover leaked through my body until I had to sit down. Jagged edges pressed through my pants, and I pushed against them, eager to be cut.

"What are you doing?" the boy asked, back at my side.

"It isn't fair to torture me," I pleaded. "You aren't real. The sunshine. The forest. Whatever the hell . . . Go away. You're leading me the wrong way anyway."

"No. I'm not." He said this with such authority that I had to look at him. The sun that had lit the imaginary field now lent him a shaft to illuminate his wholeness. His face through the windshield, I realized. Half an ear. His feet of tar from the melted street. My brother. My sweet baby brother. He let me pull him close, as sobs fought their way out of me, breaking things on the way. He stroked my head with his shattered hands, sang me a song I had lullabied him to sleep with a decade ago. "You are my hiding place. You always fill my heart, with songs of deliverance whenever I am afraid . . ."

"I'm afraid," I whispered, tears like communion into my mouth.

"It's scary," he said.

"No shit," and we both laughed at the illicit word as if we were in church. "Where have you been?" I accused. "I really could've used you."

"I'm here now." The violence of his injuries had given his face a permanence, like a marble statue in a park. Weather-beaten but stronger than nature itself.

"But you'll leave. You left me just now."

"No," and he said my name like a doctor calming a pa-tient. "I just went back for this. You dropped it. You'll need it." He handed me my rucksack. I must have left it back at the mound where I'd met him. Or maybe I hadn't taken a step at all.

"Where am I? Tell me now, in case you leave again. Or I get lost."

"You are lost." This time neither of us laughed.

"I don't want to be. I want to be home. Not home. Just away. From this." He didn't answer. His eyes, purple and perfect, said what I already knew. "I don't want to be any-where," I admitted.

"But you're here," the little boy said. Suddenly not my brother at all. Suddenly a shape without a shape. Not invisible. Not an outline but a presence, like fear or hope or faith. "Be here," the emptiness said. Gone. Then all the nothing that was left spun around my face like a veil removed. And, in a flash, I knew which way to head.

For the first time since they'd corralled me at the train station and snuck me into this endless sentence, I could feel the earth under my feet. It didn't matter that I didn't know the name of the place. I knew it was a place. Where people had lived. Where the good, the bad, and the indifferent had made a history of their own. I was treading over destroyed history. Not an idea. But something people had sweated over, dreamed of. These streets were not designed for war, which was why they were so unrecognizable. An airstrip is an airstrip is a barracks is a cell. Things built for war are not transformed by war, they are oxygenated. Enlivened. That which they are doesn't change, it only becomes effulgent.

Depending on the city, these streets had been freckled with bakeries and bookstores. Halal cafés or antique markets. I could sense that now. The destruction was uneven because nothing destroyed had been uniform. Surging condominiums had crumpled alongside squat bistros. The dead below my hurry were architects and schoolmates. Insurance men and charity workers. The homeless holding hands with diplomats. We are always one at death.

The hotel had insinuated that, but there were hotels

everywhere. Airports. Suburbs. Factory towns. This hotel revealed itself only in its ruin. Multinational cash in the safe, proximity to buildings tall enough for a sniper to hide in their skeletons, in what seemed to be a medium-to-large city. I scanned my memory for details of the hotel. An outdoor pool but no indoor one. So odds were we were somewhere hot enough to make an indoor pool redundant. The curtains in the room were heavy brocade. To black out excessive sunlight, most likely. This was a sunny place before the pollution of violence blotted out the sun. The keys to our rooms were heavy and uncopyable, so the building was probably at least fifty years old, or it had been designed to look that way. Regardless, it was luxurious, so this was a wealthy metropolis. I checked off city after city in my head, as each criterion limited the field. And I walked. I was not afraid of Mc. anymore. My brother's visit had made me feel as ethereal as he, and I gained confidence that I would sniff out Mc.'s laughing chicanery long before he had his bead on me.

Snipers' bullets remained a threat, especially considering that whoever took out my sniper was likely still out there and still eager to ice another. But deeper was the newly abiding sense that I just wasn't going to die. Not immortality — even after talking to my little brother, I didn't lean on that. If I'd believed in heaven, I'd have confessed all and gone begging for land mines. This feeling was one of temporary shelter. That wherever I moved, a shield was following. The land mine was shy. The sniper fled. The hotel burned without waiting for my reservation. I was tramping around out here for a reason, and, until I found it, no bullet could craft its way in. It was a theory I could use for cover until the heavy stuff started to fall.

That was why I wasn't afraid when I heard the singing. Why I instinctively walked toward it. It was coming from beyond what appeared to be a ridge to my left. I had yet to figure the poles, so left and right were still precious friends. The voices, and there seemed many, sang a wordless song. The harmonies were doleful, with a melody alighting atop the dirgelike foundation like a child running circles at a funeral. I keened my ear, thirsty for any language, but received only tonal beauty in return. Closer, louder. I knew soon I would either have to crawl on my belly or pull out a gun. The air threatened to clear. The ridge was a ridge of bones. And as I climbed skeletoned ribs like a ladder, the singing reached its climax. In the sick mist stood ten or more, shrouded in robes or shawls, their faces downcast. All but one held a solemn note as I bit my breath to keep from joining in. The melodist danced a soliloquy around his mouth and let it trickle out one note at a time. As if he were telling himself a secret again and again. Then he stopped.

And looked at me. Or looked at me and then stopped. It didn't matter. They all stood in sudden silence, watching me like thin wolves spying unexpected prey.

I saw then what they were praying over. A body. I had indianed up on a funeral. Their silence and immobile eyes seemed to allow for an escape, but I could not move. Because the body they were mourning should have been mine. They were grieving over my sniper.

It is possible to be so afraid that you're not afraid. Muscles clench so tightly that they become a new kind of strong. Like falling off a cliff and realizing that it isn't falling at all. It is flying. It's only the landing that changes your mind . . . so just don't land.

That was the kind of flying I was doing as I climbed up and over the ridge of bones and down toward their solemn circle. They bore a resemblance to my sniper, but whether it was familial or sympathetic I could not discern. They remained silent as I hurtled toward them. And I was running. Like a fox fleeing the hunter. It seemed vital to reach the circle, be absorbed by it, so I wouldn't be out in the terrible open anymore. I needed shelter, and, if it also meant death, then so be it. At least I would be noticed by other human beings. I wouldn't be utterly anonymous. It would count until these individuals all decided to forget. I was running like a boy returning home.

I was guessing at that emotion. The one of a child rushing home for cookies, or summer, or to be hoisted up by a parent and slingshot into joy, shoulder to shoulder, hip to knee to giggling stomach, I'm home. Home had always been a place I'd slunk into, or snuck around. I'd learned how to be a spy long before they plucked me and my anger out of my life and into this war. Time had not uncommonly found me standing behind my father with his straightedge in my hand. I could have shut him up, or at least scared the hell out of him, a hundred times. OK, maybe three. But it gave me power, knowing I could do him in if he decided to go for my mother or brother or me. I could sneak up on anything.

I sneaked into the back of a cop car once, when I was thirteen, and sat there for more than an hour. Listened to two crew cuts talk about details it would take me years to realize were about sex. I could smell their coffee and sweat through the iron mesh as they sounded stupider with each passing comment. Boo, I'd longed to say. But I knew the fun would have been rapidly replaced by an arrest and more redundant pain at home. So I let the door half open be my warning. Hid behind a Pontiac until they realized they'd not been alone. They popped out, guns drawn, expletives like firecrackers in the asphalt night. I backed away, watching them argue and investigate like chickens after an egg theft.

Down this narrow hill I ran. Was I making a sound? A clicking of my tongue, perhaps, to mimic their mourning. A hum. A sound that would be the same in any language. I didn't know what that word was.

Their hoods were not of cloth but their own hands, which were interlocked over their heads in grief. Those hands now fell to their sides. This was when they'd pull out their weapons, I realized. I pictured a dramatic demise, my bullet-pocked body stumbling its way down on top of my sniper. Dead like I should have been already. Destiny denied not a second longer.

"Stop," I heard. It was English. They did understand English. But I couldn't stop. My legs and heart were moving too fast to halt. When I was fifteen steps away from them, bones like treeless roots, turning my ankles as I came, they encircled my sniper. They thought I was attacking. They were afraid. They had brought no weapons to a funeral. No civilized man would. But we were in the fold between civilization and its discontents. They needed guns. I pulled mine.

"Stop," I said, to myself. I didn't want what I was trained to do. "Stop, goddamn it, stop!" I did. Inches from this wall of outstretched hands, this flesh barricade, fingernails for barbed wire. Flashing eyes for a silent alarm. My gun came to rest on an open palm. I put it away as an apology. "Stop," I breathed, my words pale in the new charcoal atmosphere. "I . . . stopped."

And that was enough for them. Because they began to sing again. The pinions of sorrow, dotted like i's with the pianissimo melody. And as they sang they turned back around to face the corpse, keeping me on the outside. I tried to ease closer, but they seamlessly kept me behind and blinded. Their strange tallness added to my frustration. I circled to the left and found them gently rotating in that direction. Their arms were once again above their heads, but their torsos seemed to interlock at the ribs and seal me out completely.

So I sat down. My feet demanded it. I realized they were in the kind of pain I'd read about in books about war. A feeling of being flayed from within. A condition brought on by overuse, adrenaline, and bad shoes. I longed to peel my boots like browned banana skins, but I couldn't reach them. A cramp climbed my shins, electrocuted my knees, seared my groin, and lit itself inside my belly. It was as if I'd been shot.

I looked up the moment I realized the singing had ceased. The mourners were gone. They had snuck out on me. I was the stupid cop, distracted by my pain. I could just see their outlines stuttering smoothly into the twilight. Their images made conjurable by the flames that had sprung up in front of me. My sniper was burning. The funeral was over, and now the pyre had begun to take. Whether it was a religious rite or practicality, my dark ghosts had found enough kindling to make a blaze. The smell of burning flesh wrinkled the air. My cramp worsened. I lifted my shirt to find that I had, in fact, been shot.

My sniper got me, but only because he was dead. He must've had a live round on his belt that the fire popcorned out and into me about an inch below my belly button, just beneath my SAPI. It was still sticking halfway out. I squeezed the molten blackhead and blood souped into my hands. We are made of goo, I thought. Goo and electrons. Impractical, foolish, vulnerable. And yet some of us find it extremely difficult to die. I stepped into the flames and dragged my sniper free. I thought I heard protests from the invisible far. A keening, worried cry. The mourners had noticed the silence of the fire, now denied its meal. They would be back, and this time with guns of their own.

The sniper was warmer than he had been in life, and his tendons and bones collected ash, postmortem tattoos. "Who are you?" I asked. "And I'll leave you alone. I just need to know where I am." The voices were now matched by sliding footsteps. I had only moments left with my totem. In his back pocket I found a wallet. The light was good enough to read by, but I wouldn't have the time. I jammed the wallet into my waistband, the hot leather stinging my belly wound, and lifted my sniper. He was light as a kid. The heaviness of his soul now departed, I thought. The flames took his body gracefully, leaving me unmarked. By the time the mourners returned, they found they had nothing to worry about. Their compatriot was on his way to dispersal. And the interloper was gone.

Gone, but not forgotten. I heard them fire my gun after me. I checked my belongings. Sniper's wallet, yes. My Beretta, no. My gun fired again, this time the whistle like a bully's tease beside my ear. So on ruined, disobedient feet, I ran serpentine and forward. Or backward. Wherever. I laughed as I ran. Camouflage. If there was one thing this place didn't expect, it was a genuine, hearty, tear-jerking laugh.

The first time I went to the beach was with a neighborhood family on a thunderstruck Memorial Day weekend. I was almost eleven, and, living as close to the beach as we did, I was given to make up elaborate stories of my ocean exploits in order to fend off inquiries from my tanned schoolmates every September. At five I killed a shark with a knife I held in my teeth. At seven I survived a wave that pulled me under for five, no, ten minutes. The September after my tenth birthday, I told a gripping tale of swimming with giant sea squid and schools of dolphins, etc. I figured out halfway through that this one big doozy was undoing the goodwill all the earlier stories had earned. I knew then I would have to become a better liar. I also believe that pity spawned by that story inspired little JJ to invite me to the beach with his family the following year.

JJ was the kind of boy they scouted for kid surfer-clothes advertisements. Even his freckles were blond. None of us knew at the time that drugs would poison everything sweet inside him and curdle it into cruel stupidity. In the fifth grade, JJ was the coolest, nicest kid any of us knew. JJ's parents picked me up at school that Friday (my mom had packed, or rather overpacked, a bag for me that left me staggering by the bus circle). They treated me like a regular from the moment I opened the door. JJ pummeled me. His sisters touched my thick brown hair like doctors unsure of the diagnosis. His mother smiled at me so broadly that her soapy aroma wafted back like a visible cloud. JJ's dad was losing his cherry-gray hair, and his bald spot crinkled when he spoke back over his shoulder to me. We drove, listened to music that was forbidden in my house, and did a weird number game that involved license plates, distances between towns, and somehow always guaranteed that JJ's dad won.

Before we even got to their house on the water, I decided to use whatever legal means necessary to become a member of this family for life. The house was exactly the same as every other house on the block wherever it was in whatever town. I don't remember anything about the house except that it was eighty-seven fast-running steps to the ocean. I opened the car door before we stopped, let my bag fall to the driveway beside me, and sprinted toward the foaming mouth of it like it was hungry for my dive. It wasn't until I exhaled out of a wave and looked ashore that I realized I'd gone in with all my clothes on. JJ's dad was laughing so hard his stomach shook beneath the cling of his shirt. The mom smiled and waved. And JJ peeled his pants like a healed patient peeling a bandage, and we were riding waves until the moon pushed us home. That night my breathing was shallow and my limbs ached. Maybe I was secretly a fish, I thought, and could fully breathe only in my natural habitat. Morning seemed a prison sentence away.

On Saturday it rained. The sisters stayed inside and built a dollhouse out of cereal boxes. The little brother ate the spillover and was later accused of swallowing their doll's bedroom suite. The parents stayed in their bedroom, save for forays to the cocktail cabinet. And JJ watched TV. I couldn't believe that a little water was keeping everyone from going in the water. After the fourth comedy-free cartoon in a row, and countless fruitless hints to get JJ beachside, I left my new family and ran back toward the sea. The sand was deserted, save for two enormous women under an umbrella as useless as one you'd find in a drink. They bobbed under it at intervals, rationing their dryness. Until I took them both by the hand and led them into the ocean.

Happiness. That's what it was. I didn't have a name for it, because nothing that private had ever happened to me and also brought me . . . whatever the feeling was. It was like learning a language and becoming fluent in the same day. I told jokes to the fat women. One wore a green bathing cap festooned with stars. When she came out of the water, she glistened like a Christmas tree. She also taught me how to body surf, hands like an arrow, the wave my bow, beach as target. We competed, wave after wave, until she was too tired and I was too good. We waved to each other when they left as if we'd see each other at dinner. And still it rained. In wide, silvery drops it fell like kisses, kerplunking into silence against the endless surge. The ocean canceled out the rain, made it redundant. I expected JJ and his family to scamper out any second. I checked the windows after every wave, but only saw their bored silhouettes moving like moths trapped in a parked car. So I swam, and talked to myself about how awesome a time I was having, and memorized every grain of the experience because next week's stories were not going to be lies. I didn't need a knife and a shark and a near-death experience. I had, for the first time I could remember, exactly what I needed. It was what I was doing. I was satisfied.

JJ's dad came out to get me. He wore a thin windbreaker emblazoned with ducks, and an expression that said he was sick of waiting. I'd seen it on my dad a thousand times, only my dad's patience usually lasted about half a cigarette. When we all piled into the car, I thought it was for dinner. It was only when JJ's brother yelped, "I hate the beach," that I realized we were going home. It took every inch of lip and tooth to grind the tears away. I stared out the window pretending to play the number game again. It didn't work.

"———'s crying," JJ said. It was true, but the truth can still be a betrayal. I whipped around to let him know that he had broken the code, the combination of our new friendship. His shrug said he didn't care. And that he'd be telling kids at school, too. That was the last time I had gone to the beach.

With the sniper's wallet pressing against my weeping wound, and my feet feeling slammed with every step, I suddenly found myself sinking. Every step was a dent into mud thick as clay. I couldn't see where I was, so I tried to reverse my direction. Sand again. Quicksand, I thought. A booby trap. Maybe this was Africa. This city was built on a jungle. I panicked only to fall deeper. I was now up to my knees, each lift and separation taking strenuous effort. My heart pounded in my belly. Blood crawled warm across and down onto my hips like a wide spider. I finally couldn't lift my second leg and keeled forward onto my hands. I grabbed for the wallet to keep it above the suction of the earth. Useless and exhausted. I yielded and lay my face down onto the surface as my hands were sinking, too. Up to my elbow. This is how I will go, I thought. Neither victor nor vanquished. Just an unfinished sentence swallowed by the mouth of earth. Then it kissed my lips. Weakly, shy as a good-night. There was no aroma. The air was crow-black and smelled of the dead and their killers. Another kiss. Wetter. Saltier. Happiness, I thought. This isn't the earth. This is the sea.

I crawled toward the lick of water, the sand taking me deeper. I couldn't hear how far and was too excited to stop and wait for it. All I heard was the slog and pop of my hands and knees in and out of the wet sand. I even forgot to care that the sniper's wallet had disappeared in one of the sinkholes about three crawls back. I was moving toward something primal and perfect. There would be no violence in the ocean.

At the moment I found my first wave, tiny as a wicket, it didn't seem to matter that the planet was awash in coastlines and that my search for place was no further along. What mattered was that I was eleven again, JJ was stuck in the house with his tipsy parents, and I was free.

I took off my shirt. And undid my vest, the porcelain too heavy for a swim. I tossed it and my ruck just out of the water's stretch. The salt water burned its healing into my wound, and I splashed it until the bleeding was finally done. The sea was tepid as the third child's bath, but it offered a sudden gathering of waves, which I could now hear and therefore surf. I caught the first one poorly, the white water leaving me behind in a tight-fisted curl of foam . . . I clambered back out again, chesting against the late breakers and diving under the taller rips. Out deeper, the water was colder, and I realized the residue of the fighting had turned the ocean's edge into a stew, but nothing could affect its color and speed closer to its source. I was past standing now, and though the sky was choked black, I could sense the moon above me, pulling at the tide with a puppeteer's grace.

I turned onto my back, floating to gaze at the chalkboard above me. Not a mark. Not an equation of light. I imagined for a moment that I hadn't heeded JJ's father's call. That instead of hurrying (reluctantly) toward his elbowed gesture, I had simply ducked under and vanished. Would anyone have even cared? Of course there would've been a search party. The police. But only to assuage the guilt JJ's parents had at bringing a stranger. They wouldn't be out looking for me. It would be an APB for their peace of mind. Their suburban calm. Their place in the world.

It might have been easy. Catch the tiger by the undertow and, holler or not, never let go. Surf it to a distant southern village where they cooked on the beach and welcomed mer-boys like tourists welcoming birds back for a season. I could've been their mascot. Their sign that summer had come, and, upon seeing me, the fish would jump in their boats without a hook for an invitation. But I hadn't. I'd obeyed the bitter rhythm of my days and wound up back in my house in time to hear my father mock my tears. My mother offered comfort by telling me that was why she never took us to the beach. Leaving was too disappointing. Better not to go at all.

It took a war to get me back to the beach. The hotel had been a seaside resort. That explained the outdoor furniture. The beach chairs and clamshells painted on the bottom of the pool. The pool was undersized, too, because the real thing was so close. I'd never seen a view, with the blackout-curtain sealant, but I wagered my corner room might have had a straight shot to the horizon. Maybe a terrace where the wind was meant to unfurl like a countryless flag. A symbol of nothing but itself. The beauty of something brought to life only when the wind decided to blow.

I dove under, holding my breath longer than I should have, then rose, light-headed and weak. Again. I wasn't trying to drown. Suicide was never the point. I didn't have enough of a self to want to erase. But the pain and the danger felt good. If I couldn't have an enemy out this deep, I'd make one of oxygen. Again and again, until surfacing wasn't an act of will but a science, the remaining air in my lungs making my body buoyant enough. Finally, I floated again. I was punishing myself for being happy in the water. For wanting to play, not just in the middle of a war, but in the middle of my life.

I floated again because I was too tired to swim. And the current had taken me out past the waves, so the beach was no longer an option. Water swam in and out of my ears like lazy midday traffic through a tunnel. I listened to the metronome of my brain in my temples. The ocean held me up and around, and for the first time in . . . I felt safe. It didn't matter how far out I was. The ocean was telling me, "I will hold you until." Until didn't matter. It would be the exact moment of time.

Something brushed my arm. I let it bob up against and around. Driftwood, seaweed, a body, I didn't want to know. This was my time. No one got to call me in. No one.

"Hey, ————," I heard Mc. shout from the beach. His voice sounded like burning leaves. "Get the fuck out of the water."

Of course I knew it wasn't Mc. Even in my blissed-out state, with water music in my ears, I didn't think he could have spotted me adrift in all that darkness.

"Son," I heard my father say, "no joke. Ass in." That had been his standard threat if I was too long in the yard before dinner. And it had always sounded like a joke to me. Ass in. So I'd walk, awkward as a chicken, ass in, toward the door he would have already abandoned. He never expected needing to say it twice. Though that night, from the distant beach, he did parrot. "No joke. Ass in."

"It *is* a joke," I said, rising to a sitting position. I stretched my legs to feel the bottom. Not even close.

"No joke." I could see his convex gut, his lit cigarette like a tiny, sideways lighthouse.

"Go home, Dad. Go back in your hole."

"OK," he said. Then flicked his smoke into a wave. Gone.

What makes a man a soldier? Is it only war, or is there a collection of tiny hatreds along the way that grow like pylons inside the soul? A foundation for better hatreds to be poured onto in adolescence. Alienation. Projection. Disassociation, even for the self. Was the blighted seascape peopled only by men like me? Men hallucinating their fathers and destroyers? Men perfectly suited to kill until they died? Or were there good souls out here? Men of honor and tenderness, snatched by the times? Posted on street corners, shivering with fear and want of their wives?

It was possible that my sniper was such a man, but he wasn't around to ask. His wallet may have contained photos of family. Children in sports uniforms, dogs in the back. A library card. A bank card. A stub for the movies. If I had stayed in the water that long-ago day (found a new family, slipstreamed into a different life), might I have had such a wallet?

I'd never get to know. Because I didn't get to stay in the water. The sea wouldn't let me. A cocktail of wave and tide lifted me like a jellyfish and deposited me flat on the sand. Then it receded. The sand was soft again. The ocean undressed itself of me and left me undrowned on the beach.

I was wrong. There was someone on the beach. He yanked me to my feet and hooked me under the armpit to walk me out of there. "Hey," I said.

"You were out there a long time," he said. His voice was as familiar as a hymn.

"Didn't want to come back."

"Don't blame ya." His "ya" was without any forced hominess. This was a man who said "ya" and couldn't say otherwise.

"Where are we going?" I asked. "What time is it? Where are we?" The questions came in a little boy's comic burst.

"We'll get ya there," and his answer seemed enough. The fact that he was carrying me seemed to merit deference and patience anyway. "Could've drowned out there. Shouldn't drift out so deep."

"Drifting." I laughed. "Is what I do best." Gunfire. First bullets, like stones skipped over a lake. Then mortar rounds. Five hits lit up the mark enough to highlight toppled cars and road signs like tall, dead birds. He hunched us lower and sped us on. "I can walk," I said.

"Not as fast as me."

"Where . . . ?"

"Toward the sun," he explained. "Can't see nothing out here but bodies and tracers that want to turn us into bodies."

"R.?" He didn't answer, but I knew it was him. He had survived Mc.'s ambush. Maybe he'd known a secret place to hide. In the yard, of course, or the subbasement. The king always knows where to hide during a coup. He'd hidden and gotten out before I'd even found the wreckage. And I had miscounted the casualties. We were moving faster now, and there was a thin band of light in the distance, like an old TV set trying to turn on. "R," I said, using my feet more, trying to help carry my own weight. "I've been looking for Mc."

"No, you haven't, bleeder. You were taking a goddamn swim." He turned then, and the half-light revealed his classic grim smile. It also showed he hadn't completely escaped the force of Mc.'s treachery. His left eye was sealed shut, with stripes of metal still visible beneath the skin of his cheek and chin. I should have been hoisting him.

"You have to brief me, sir," I shouted. The gunfire was getting closer and louder. "I can help. I'm not a bleeder any-more." He was. A round caught him hard and clean through the left shoulder, spinning him around so that he was now on the other side of me and I had my chance to carry him.

"Goddamn it," he cowboyed. It sounded as if he blamed himself for having flesh to wound.

"Point, sir. We've got to get out of this fire." He didn't answer. I knew the wound wasn't mortal, so I added to my push. "R., soldier to soldier, tell me safe haven. Tell me the map."

"Safe haven," he laughed.

"You were running me somewhere," I barked, still moving forward.

"Anywhere, soldier. Not somewhere." It was mine. They talked about this briefly in training. When the chain of command is broken through injury or death, the situation will become mine. Possession. Like an inheritance. Or a family curse. But with R. listing and already ugly with loss, it had to be mine or death was going to be ours.

The white band of light had risen to the occasion, and it gave me enough vision to see a triangle of metal structures about a hundred yards up a rise to our right. Office buildings. Maybe an arena long disassembled by smart bombs. I flashed on cities that had sports stadiums near the ocean. Like the hell I know. "Check the internet," I said to myself out loud.

Before I could laugh, R. said, "You think everything's funny, don't ya?"

I hooked my hand into R.'s belt and rocketed us up the ridge faster than either of us expected. Bullets chased us like kids late for a bus. It was officially morning. Flat light hummed a cold wave off the dangling metal forest we'd entered. Exposed wires. Infrastructure. I slinked us deeper in, listening for fainter guns and looking for crevices for foxholes. Found myself counting. "Forty-one, forty-two," I enunciated quickly, careful not to miscount.

"Hell ya doing?"

"Shut up, sir. I'm getting to eighty-seven." Eighty-seven steps into the rib cage of former commerce, there was a hallway nearly untouched. All the surface amenities had burned away, of course. There was no carpeting, furniture, water cooler, fax. But the shape was uncompromised. The bullets had turned their attention elsewhere. I looked back on our trail, and it seemed appropriately difficult to follow. I imagined having a hell of a time getting back out. But for the moment it looked sufficient. I turned R. so he could take in the entire area. We looked like business partners about to launch a start-up. "What do you say, R.?"

"I think we should take it," he allowed, his tone saying thank you.

"OK," I agreed, easing him down and tearing open his sleeve. He gestured toward the knife in his belt, and I tested the entry point. He was lucky. It had passed clean through. "But I get the corner office. Why are we at war?" I shifted, hoping to surprise an answer out of him.

"Because the government says so."

"Which government?"

"Do you forget where ya come from, boy?"

"It seems I do."

"The goddamn United States of America."

"United by what?"

"Don't get political, bleeder. Fighters fight, thinkers think." In the gathering light, I could see better how ruined his face was. Blind in one eye, for sure, with metal polyps studding his face like tribal markings. I bandaged his wound just to look away.

"Who are we fighting, sir?"

"Everyone now. Everyone with a gun. This place is chaos. We just need to get out alive. That's why I came after you. You're the last of my unit. Need to bring someone home."

"Mc.'s alive."

"Possible."

"I'm not going back until I find him."

R. grunted and rose. His gait wobbled and he leaned against me for balance, then pushed off with bravado. I had to catch that fall.

"You need to lie down, sir. You're out of blood."

"Can't shoot what you can't see." I didn't know if he meant us or Mc.

"He was a traitor. No one can prepare for that," I said, feigning wisdom with my tone but believing it, too.

"I should have seen it. He was too goddamn loud. Even his hair was a fucking shout." The image drew a laugh, and R. coughed one back at me. "Guess I ain't too pretty no more."

"It's all right," I lied.

"No it ain't. But it'll have to be. Besides, my wife never bothered much with that." I got R. propped up against a rerouting pipe, with his rucksack as pillow, and he closed his eyes.

"Where are we, sir?" No answer. I felt weak from ignorance. I pondered beating it out of him, whatever it took. "Sir?"

"I don't know."

"Don't bullshit me," I growled. "There's no reason left to. No mission. You want to bring me back in, and you're too sick to walk. You need to tell me, sir. R. Tell me now."

Eyes still closed, he said, "I don't know."

I dropped to my knees, metal digging in through my pants, and slapped him hard. My teeth felt like biting the shrapnel out of his face. "You're going to tell me, because I can't not know anymore, you understand? I'm not fucking around."

"Neither am I. And you're hurting my shoulder." I reared back to punch him. Recalled what I did to Y. and how easy it would be to do again. I could aim for the windpipe, give him a real reason to keep quiet. "Don't," he said, eyes still shut. "I can't hurt any more right now."

"Then say it."

"I did. Word never came down. I was transported in just like you. Blindfold. Orders in code. I couldn't tell you if this was Tokyo or Bangladesh."

"I don't believe you."

"Doesn't matter. I can't tell you, either way." I wanted to throw him back against the pipe but found myself laying him down gently as a nurse. "Thanks, kid. For not doing what you do." Violence, he meant. That's what I did. What I was known for.

"Why did you send me out? Before . . ."

"Luck, I guess, for you. You got luck." He opened his good eye, and it made him look like he was letting me in on a joke. "Anything else you want to know?" We both laughed again, short, snorting laughs that didn't satisfy.

"When's Christmas?" I asked.

"December twenty-fifth, last time I checked," he managed.

"I mean how close? To today."

"Maybe Santa could pick ya up." His breath shortening. "Hell of a wait, bleeder. Can't be later than end of summer." I stood up and walked ten feet toward where we had arrived from. Stuck out my tongue. It wasn't ash.

"Then, sir, why is it starting to snow?"

R. didn't respond. I guess he was tired of questions he couldn't answer. I went to check to make sure the bastard hadn't died on me, and he smirked, "Go play in the snow. Bleeder."

I explained I wanted to check the perimeter, see if I could get a better grasp on the landscape, but I really did just want to play in the snow. Combat was having a bizarre effect on me, it was bringing out the boy. I saw the tangled remains of the office building as a metal fort that needed exploring. As I tiptoed room to room, I wasn't half as afraid as I should've been. I kept waiting for little brother to pop out again and take me to the hill where there'd be enough accumulation to make a snowman. He'd always been a brilliant snowman constructor, even as I'd pelt him with snowballs from the roof. "I'm coming," I would yell, drilling him everywhere but the off-limits ears.

But there was no little brother that morning. Just me and my curiosity. How in the hell could it be snowing? I'd heard of seasonal cold snaps all over the world. It had snowed in deserts, on beaches, in the middle of a lake near my hometown when I was less than ten. It snowed like a funnel over a half-mile radius of the water, while not an inch fell anywhere outside of it. And the lake left the mystery proofless by absorbing every flake. Yet all those events shared one element that this day did not. It had been cold. And as I reached out my hand to feel the cool tingle of a landing flake, steam rose off my skin because it was so summertime hot.

I patrolled the entire floor we were on and saw that I could follow a path of half steps and melded elevator shafts to the floors above. There was no roof, and the higher I climbed, the faster and thicker the snow fell. I could still see the top of R.'s head. The flakes disappearing into his hair looked like tiny mice burrowing into the earth.

Farther up and in I traveled, needing my hands to purchase balance. Looking up toward the building's severed head, my eyesight yielded to what was fast becoming a deluge. Small hills of white formed on my shoulders and boot tops. The higher I climbed, the calmer I felt. Snow made everything all right. It covered over the scars of November and whited out whole days of school. There was a reason to go outside and not respond till the dinner bell. Snow meant sledding on garbage-can lids and pushing little brother down hills inside of the garbage can (garbage included, preferably), which inevitably left him covered in cabbage and laughing uncontrollably. Snow salad, we called it, and we couldn't get enough. It meant Dad stuck in the driveway and brother and me pushing till our veins were outside our skin. Laying down salt, shoveling, all while he gunned the exhaust. Because we needed him off at work, not stuck at home ruining our snow day.

By the time I realized how high I'd climbed, I couldn't see R. anymore. The snow was sideways and wide, and I had little visibility to go higher. It took a shiver to tell me I was cold. A bracelet of wires around the bony wrists of remaining concrete was frozen over. The snow wasn't coming from the sky above. It was coming from this floor.

A snowmaker? Not countless floors up in a city high-rise. That was for mountain resorts, for the rich to outwit the weather. It was windy too, and my footing gave way like an awkward skater's. Memories shoved down and vanished as I walked toward the unknowable again. As I remembered I was at war. Whatever that meant. But it did mean strangers wished me ill. Unseen strangers. And that man had invented ten thousand ways to kill, and if this was one I hadn't seen before, then all the better to kill me with. I tasted the passing snow. Tongued it for traces of poison, as if I could discern.

The chill was so confusing and my steps so uneasy that I didn't know I'd reached the source until I'd gotten there. My hand touched freezing metal. Went to scrape off a ramp of snow and got burned. Not frostbite. The burn of a searing-hot cauldron took three layers of fingertip and palm before I could pull away.

I swallowed my scream, now certain I was in enemy territory, and slipped down below the snow. I was flat on my back, looking up at a blizzard shooting out above me. My hand scissored with pain. I jammed it into a mound of snow to soothe it. Instead, the snow melted, and the burn raged.

What was it coming out of, a hole in the side of the sky? I slid backward under the snow, and within moments the floor was firm. No ice! No chill. And no blinding blizzard.

In front of me was a two-hundred-fifty-pound bomb nestled like a baby in the manger of the building's cooling system. A dangerous baby. Because the bomb had not exploded yet.

Its thermal-heated core was still cooking. And its proximity to the building's enormous rooftop cooling system, still operating on fail-safe despite loss of power, had created its own front. War makes weather, too, I thought, darkly impressed. War is the ultimate possessor. War doesn't destroy. It makes everything else into war.

I looked at my hand. The skin was purple with visible capillaries pumping like trapped insects in my fingertips. Part of my palm was missing from heel to thumb. I could see the snow was growing thinner on the other side. The bomb was heating. It would reach climax no matter how cool its target appeared to be.

Run. *Run*, I barked at myself, but I couldn't. This swollen bomb, hungry to burst, was as mesmerizing as the sun. I wanted to see it rip open, throw its seeds across the white-sick air. I didn't want to die, just see how this piece of metal fruit made people die. Who built this? What engineer dreamed it, craftsmen formed it, politician celebrated it, taxpayer funded its mass production, allocation, and ultimately its definition . . . boom. It was formed to come apart. Obsolescence in its own circular perfection. I stared, a visitor to the museum of this war. I'd paid for my ticket. I wanted to see the finale.

Then the bomb practically lifted its skirt and revealed itself to me. It had been covered in its own snow, but the heat
was so intense now, the floor felt like cheese beneath me. It
was the country's flag above the weight demarcation. Three
colors I had memorized in my training, but in sixth-grade
geography class, not at the hotel. And then below the flag,
another tattoo silvered into view. This one read "Made in the
U.S.A." That finally got me to run.

Back down through the snow, which was now more like
sleet, slicking every surface. I fell into a tangle of wires, then
shoulder first into a rebar so bent it appeared to be flexing
its bicep. Metal pinched and tore at me, leaving fresh gashes
and welts. Beautiful by the pool, I told myself. So many stories to tell. Just get down, get R., and have a mouth left to
tell them with. But how many flights had I climbed? The
building accordioned up at me, and, despite minutes of
rapid descent, I still couldn't see my C.O.

The snow was now rain down this low. And the sun
muscled farther up over the weighted horizon. Four seasons
in one day. "R.!" I yelled, not afraid to draw fire now. This
entire block would be barbequed before anybody could get
lucky with a shot. "R.!"

"What?" He turned, only fifteen feet away. "The hell
ya yelling for?" The melted snow had flattened his hair to
his head. He looked like a middle-aged man in the middle
of a haircut. I didn't have time to explain, so I rag-dolled

him up and squeezed his wounded wing to ensure he obeyed.

"Bomb," I said, and then he was helping, too. We scrambled back the way we'd entered, even though it had been a hot spot hours before.

"Size?"

"Two-fifty."

"Shit."

We scrambled out, and as soon as we cleared the first line of vision, the bullets started. "Don't these fuckers have anything better to do?" R. bellowed. He sounded like my father stuck in traffic. "You're all gonna die, assholes," as a bullet whizzed by my ear loud enough to scare out the wax. We stayed low, serpentined, did everything the good book said, and it was working. The shooters were missing like drunks at a carnival.

"There's always one duck they miss, soldier," R. growled, in sync with my thoughts. "Let's be that duck." Faster, and now it seemed I was hanging on to R. for my sake, not his. We shimmied and shook like athletes on television.

"Are we aiming for something?" I asked. Up ahead there appeared to be a clutch of former structures that could possibly provide cover. I couldn't name any one in particular, because the rubble had a sameness to it.

"Preacher's hat," R. said.

"Which one is that?" I sputtered. "And what the hell is that?"

"Pope, who gives a shit?" Then I saw it. A tall, thin shaft shaped like the pontiff's hat, as if the landscape were giving us the finger. We angled for it, bullets still stupid in their aim. Just outside the pope's hat we realized it was a tractor-trailer full of unsold Japanese cars. The trailer had been blown up onto its nose, and white plaster and bomb dust covered everything in a pale patina. The cars on the trailer were all glassless but aside from that showed little damage. Even the tires appeared intact. "This ain't it," R. said as we took shelter from the barrage and tried to catch our breath.

I looked back toward the building we'd fled. A salvo pinged off the cars and flattened several tires. Our temporary hideout swayed from the hit. "I guess we're not driving out of here."

"Your funny isn't," R. spat, and we were on the move again. The shooters must have been reloading, because we ran for a football field without a sound. I couldn't believe my hand hurt so much. It's just a fucking hand, I thought. I wanted to cut it off. Every time I looked at it, vomit suctioned up my throat.

"I have to stop," I said, puking before my feet had planted. I hadn't eaten in so long that only bile and blood trickled from my lips like spit-out medicine. "Sorry."

"Saw your hand. You touch it?" I nodded as another wave humpbacked me to my knees. "Can't wait here."

"I'm coming." But I was going.

Before I could rise, the bomb blew, and so did we. Into the air, about forty yards. The flying was in slow, then fast, then too-fast motion. In the beginning I could see the two of us lift off the ground like birds in a dream. But those birds were light, and we had weight. Weight to be lifted, carried, and thrown. Since I'd been bent over, my flight was low to the ground. I could have touched the earth if my reactions had been my own. Levitation, I thought, amazed at my own trick until I went ribs-first into the one standing light pole on the street. I felt my organs force forward like kids in the backseat. And then I was down, breathless but alive. Oh, yeah. My hand stopped hurting. R. had been ripcorded up and then slid down the air in the shape of a horseshoe. He landed with a gentle crunch, like he'd been practicing all his life. It probably took him ten minutes, but by the time I watched him limp up to me, he already seemed all right. He knelt beside me, with a wry grin. "No more snipers," he said.

It was the brightest day since I'd entered the hotel. "What caught fire?" I asked. "There's nothing left to burn." R. didn't answer, just checked my vitals, wiped blood off my face, bandaged my hand. His silence made me feel safe, and the distant aftermath of the bomb lent a tropical tinge to the warm air. "Hope it wasn't nuclear."

"Is my face melting off?" R. deadpanned.

"Your funny isn't," I mocked. Survival was always the soldier's best social elixir. "Is it all right to be in the open?"

"Whoever's left is tending to their wounded. No fighting for a breather."

"Sometimes it takes a bomb to stop the war," I said. "Sounds like a campaign slogan." R. didn't answer. "I think it was one."

"It will be now."

I wanted to tell him about the flag. And who made the bomb. If ever there was a time for a grunt to trust command, this was it. "I touched the bomb," I offered.

"No shit." R. was staring at the fires, looking for any details the added light might shed. He checked the sky. His broken watch. He stayed by my side, but he let his mind tether out like a weather balloon.

"I saw," I said. R. still didn't move, but his silence said the camaraderie was over. He either knew or didn't want to know what was etched into the skin of the bomb. But he didn't want to walk like a coward. So he stood there, close, and dared me not to say.

"Five minutes, soldier," he finally ordered. "Can't leave our shining asses out here all day." R. limped away, straightening with every step. And I sat there, my ribs splintered, my hand beginning to burn again. And my mouth shut.

The detonation and its effects allowed R. and me to walk instead of run. Although we were still in a war zone, the bomb had brought an almost pastoral calm to the area. Since we had felt its impact so severely at our distance, we knew that whoever had been chasing us was no longer able to. And if the direction we were heading held hostile forces, better to tiptoe in than announce our presence like Christian carolers or paper boys.

Walking like this, with R. a few steps ahead like my father looking for where he parked our car, I felt strangely attached to him. Not that correlating him to my father accomplished that; that should have made him feel as alien to me as cop to criminal. Rather, it was the boldness in his step, his refusal to limp despite the seep of blood visible through his pant leg. It was the walk of a leader. It was what, back at the hotel, we had all longed for without requesting. Most men yearn for nothing more than shoulder blades to follow. Into a forest, across a trafficked street, authority feeling authoritative only as it walks away. Maybe I hadn't liked R. at the hotel because he was never leading me anywhere. His bullets on The Run did inspire me in certain directions, but away from him, not toward. This walk, into the fire-bright unknown, felt like it was leading somewhere. And from three steps behind I could pretend he knew where that somewhere was.

Because of the light, I could make out several fresh details of the landscape. There were innumerable former automobiles, their thinned bodies jammed into the concrete like needles into a vein. The street was sick with them, and they were standing up so perfectly perpendicular, they appeared to have been dropped from a height. As we passed one, the trunk popped open, a gasp of hot air for hello. I turned my gun on it with paranoid speed, while R. never looked back. "Gotta learn, bleeder," he said, "to be scared of the right things."

"This isn't your first war," I defended myself.

"Don't make it your last." R. walked on, his pace slowing enough that I was catching up to him. So I slowed. I needed those shoulders to lead. And they did, guiding us left, farther away from the sea and the bomb. Within minutes we were in the most residential section I had encountered since quitting the hotel. There weren't houses, of course. Barely the L of a scooped-out apartment complex. But the streets were strewn with personal items. Proof of lives.

I found a mailbox with a bright painting of a hummingbird. The bird practically glowed green and blue against the char of the metal box. The family name was melted away, but part of the number remained. 23. 23 what? Heliostrasse? Or maybe it was 2375 Al Sadr Street. 1231 rue d'Avignon. 231 Ramsallah. 237 Victory Lane. That was the street where I'd grown up, the name mocking all my defects. We'd moved into 714 Victory Lane when I was ten. It was an ugly house on a beautiful street, daring the new owner to tear it down. But the more my mother protested the faux wood and the aluminum siding, the more my father dug in. He liked ugly things. Helped to camouflage him. By the time I moved out, not a tile had been lifted. Not a shutter painted. It remained a stab in the heart of a beautiful neighborhood. It could have used an explosive renovation like this.

But this street, with its hummingbird survivor, deserved better. Each step took us deeper into family histories. A piano, cracked and cooked like lobster, held a family photo in the crook of its broken leg. The pewter frame had survived. The faces of the four family members all burned away, just like their futures. I could guess from the bodies of the photographed it was mother, father, daughter, son. Which one played the piano? Or had this photo been exhaled from the lungs of a house two blocks away? War brought people together, blood like glue, but only in death. The living just kept getting driven further and further apart.

R. barked for me to keep up, sensing my lag from the fade of my footsteps. He never bothered to turn around. "Leave it, soldier." His voice now fifteen steps away. "It's all gone."

Yet it wasn't. I found a chair literally unscathed, its dark oak color not stained that way by ash but original. I sat in it, and it held me like a parent's arms. In front of it sat a stack of CDs that had congealed into a block of unplayable music. On either side were hand imprints where a teenager had probably tried to grab the collection, only to be burned away. I hoisted the chair over my shoulder and walked toward the shimmering image of R. up ahead. I thought, Anything that survives this shit is good luck. And it sat good. So when we did take a break, I'd have something solid beneath me. Or a gift to offer R. He'd probably laugh, call me bleeder, then take the chair.

Twenty feet ahead there was a wall that had refused to fall. It had yellow wallpaper with flecks of black and orange that might have been charred flesh and blood instead of a designer's whim. In the middle of the wall, just off-center, was the outline of a body. Like the Shroud of Turin. Soaked right through the essence of the wall. The outline was smaller than me but most likely a man's. Arms outstretched but not comedically like in a cartoon when the duck passes through rock and beam unharmed. This wall seemed to have drawn the man into itself. Absorbed him. Soaked itself with him, a possession. I touched the surface, and it was wet. Damp. But only inside the outline. I ran to the other side of the wall, but the outline wasn't visible. It was as though the man were still inside the wall.

I set the chair down and pressed my ear to the flesh of the wall. The moisture made me shudder. "Hello?" I whispered, shy to be this crazy even in front of myself. I scanned for R., but he had disappeared over a swell of wreckage. I listened again. "Hello?" I took my boot knife, aiming for a rim just beyond the outline of the body. And began to cut.

The paper gave way like fruit skin, but the drywall clutched at my knife uncooperatively. It was tiring work, and my body bloomed sweat. "What are you doing?" I asked myself. I knew my delay could mean losing R. Abandoning my commanding officer and dashing what may have been my best chance at survival. Yet something compelled me to cut.

It was just around the elbow that the body fell through. It leaned out all at once, pinning me with horror and suddenness, until I found myself on the ground, looking up into a man's open eyes. My instinct was to thrust him off, but I'd gone digging for this mummy. I was responsible for its care. Yet it wasn't a mummy.

"Did it work?" he asked. Then quietly closed his eyes.

R. was long gone. Because he had assumed I would follow his lead and his order to catch up, he had never bothered to check. That would have been a dent in his leadership confidence and he could not allow that, but this wasn't a game of pool. Sink your shot, but only after figuring out your next four shots. This was the situation. Deal with it or die. Or someone will die, either way. This wasn't rational behavior. This was a hundred-and-fifty-pound man, his beard burned off down to the pincushion surface, asleep on my chest. I gently rolled him over and surveyed his damage.

Along with his whiskers and his eyebrows, most of his clothes had been incinerated. Patches of cotton and acrylic adhered to his skin as if he were trying to quit several addictions at once. His shoes had melted around his feet, making them as curved and brown as hooves. He appeared less a man than a giant baby, cut from the womb and laid on this unclean floor as welcome. But he wasn't crying. He was barely breathing.

I wiped away a baker's fist of drywall and dust from his mouth and began resuscitation on his breathless mouth. Every inhalation tasted like steak. We're animals, I thought. Reduced to elements, we are animals. But an animal wouldn't do this. Attempt rescue. Foolishly. Put himself second and the mystery first. Animals do only what they must, they never do what they shouldn't. That was the heart then. Foolishness. That was why I could worry about R., forget myself, and try to spit life back into this burn victim. OK. But it was also selfish. This man knew what street we were on. He had answers, despite beginning our meeting with a question. He knew things I was hungry for, so I was going to yank him awake at least until I felt safer. Was that animal? Or was that just humanity at its best and worst, wed?

I took a break, light-headed from overthinking and over-breathing. The man seemed to take it as an insult and opened his whiteless eyes. We stared at each other. I couldn't tell who was more afraid. Now that his face was cleaner, I could see that he was Caucasian. I repeated his one sentence in my head — "Did it work?" — and could not detect an accent.

"Did what work?" I asked. He stared at me harder, scanning through possibilities and angles. He was a man smart enough to hide inside a wall to avoid death. He probably had a few other tricks up his sleeve. I realized that I was straddling him, his legs hemmed in by mine. But his hands were free, and, if he had the strength or lunacy, he could attack.

"Why?" His voice was thick with phlegm but louder than expected. Why what? I thought. Who is this asshole asking questions? I'm the one with questions. I just saved his goddamn life. But I kept my mouth quiet and watched the confusion in his eyes rise like water in a bathtub. I adjusted my hold on him with my thighs, remained silent. What was I doing? I saved him to intimidate him? My actions confounded me. I needed him to explain them to me, but my tongue refused to utter any requests.

"Don't die," I finally muttered.

"OK," he said, a bit forced. As though this accent-free accent he had was a put-on. As though even now, on death's driveway, he was playing a part. He turned his head to each side, taking in the space where there had been none before. He began to mumble to himself. Silently, like a prayer.

"Are you . . . You aren't from here," I investigated. He kept praying. It was in a foreign language. "You're hiding. This isn't your home." His prayer became louder, the language as foreign and insistent as water on a rock. "Stop praying!" I yelled. "I already saved you." He stopped. Looked up at me. I suddenly wanted to fill his partially open mouth with dirt instead of air. Where was R.? Why hadn't he come back to get my idiot self?

"There is a picture over by the door," he rasped. "Where the door used to be."

"Who are you?" My words died just after my lips, with nothing to echo them.

"I can see it from here, the edge of the frame. Get it."

"I'm not going," I said, impudent as a child. "You will talk."

"The picture says it." His breathing became erratic. I wanted to punch him into obedience. Instead I leaned in to give him more mouth-to-mouth. His hand caught my chest inches from contact. "I'm a peacekeeper," he whispered. "I didn't live here, until —"

"Peacekeeper." I laughed, my sweat dripping onto his. "Well, I'm a warkeeper. And it looks like we're winning." Hatred welled up in me. The hatred of the wrong, screaming useless to be right.

"I am Dutch." His accent sounded clearer suddenly, the way things seem obvious as soon as they're explained.

"What were you praying for?"

"I don't know." He coughed. "I was just praying. What I was praying before you found me. Something I remember from childhood." His mention of childhood weakened me like a last cocktail. Our violence as men took us all back to that same backyard, fort of towels and chairs, sun falling, lemonade waiting, it's-never-going-to-end guarantee in our bellies, sunk in deeper than a hook in a fish. And then we get catapulted ashore. Unsafe. Wounded. Adult.

"Will you pray it for me?" I requested, rising up above him, granting his legs freedom.

"OK," he said, "yes." As he prayed, the words landing on unexpected syllables and glottal intonations, I walked toward where he had gestured. Where the door used to be. His prayer was inscrutable, but I could tell it was the one he'd been reciting before. So if it was his prayer, he was truly offering it up for me as well.

I stepped over the soggy carpet and a fused bed frame, its gnarled bottom snarling up at me. Past the remains of a desk, a crystal lamp nestled in the ashes like a chickless hen. I barely had to lean over to pick the picture up. The randomness of destruction had decided to leave this one image be. The photo was of my wall hider in his peacekeeping uniform. His name tag read V., and he looked too handsome to go to war. Like an actor photographed for a role. The safety of a soundstage promised. The glitter of a premier and a costar's lipstick. Not real blood. Not a stolen face.

"That's who I was," he said loudly.

I walked back to him, feeling friendly all over again. His prayer was going to work. If he was here long enough to hang a picture, then he must know the land a bit. Finding R. would be easier. I wasn't lost. I just needed to find. And here was my prize. A Dutch gentleman who was smart enough to hide inside a wall.

By the time I reached him, he seemed both a genius and a friend. I angled the chair and hoisted him up into it, his body lightened by my refreshed enthusiasm. I set the picture on his lap and closed his fingers around it. Enough to guarantee it wouldn't drop. By that time, I understood that he was dead. I knelt before him and gazed into his blank eyes.

"Thank you for praying for me, V.," I said. "It's going to work." A cruel shoulder of wind tried to topple V., but I held him fast. When it subsided, so did the warmth. A chill moved wide across the land and the firelight fevered up, then dampened down. I looked off in the direction R. had marched. Looked back and could begin to see the insectlike resurrection of the enemy, out from under the boot of the bomb. Cockroaches, I thought. These assholes refuse to die.

But so did I. What did that make me? Was that animal? Or was that luck? I kissed V.'s head like he was the pope himself and decided it made me neither. If the dead were praying for me, maybe the living wouldn't know where to look. And whether that was luck or a miracle, I didn't care. Not as I ran after the hope of R. on the faith of V. I'm a cockroach, motherfucker. Here I come.

R. wasn't where I imagined. Time had turned against me, and the darkness encroached like a second army. I was moving at a clip, keeping my footsteps as silent as a soldier can. Deeper into the former residential area I went, looking for any pile of remains where R. might be resting or awaiting my arrival so as to give me a hell of a razzing. I looked forward to it. To him caring enough to yell. To telling him about V. Maybe the presence of peacekeepers would narrow down our list of locales.

I'd never had any desire for friends before the war. My patience for small talk didn't last past a bowl of peanuts, two beers, and a quarter of football. It was a combination of disinterest in my fellow humans and an absolute certainty that I had nothing to say that wouldn't lead to anger and the threat of fists. My silence was an act of mercy, or that was the lie I told myself. Even at the hotel, aside from listening to Mc.'s horseshit, which always went down better in a group, I rarely fraternized. None of us did. We'd been chosen for being antisocial. We had trouble sitting in a room together without the vibrating promise of violence. Yet here the real fighting was turning me into a man in need of a friend. If V. had lived, I'd probably still be back at the half house, swapping stories and dreaming of Amsterdam. Now I wanted nothing more than R.'s face, a chance to pass the night hidden from view and open to conversation.

I was beginning to embarrass myself with these new inclinations. There are things we don't give ourselves permission to think. Ideas of identity that we have so successfully and attentively constructed that the notion of toppling them, even for the best of reasons, seems blasphemous. Number one on the shrine of self was the commandment "I do not need." Need was weakness and weakness was death. But strength was death out here, too. All the former symbols and rituals had failed me. I needed, yes, needed new markers, flags planted at the edge of me. And if someone was there to help me plant the flag, it would only dig down deeper.

Maybe that was V.'s prayer working in me. He had come to keep peace. Of course, he'd brought a gun, but at least his mission bore a name that sounded like hope. Peace, hope, love. Hah. Now I was truly going soft. I needed to grit up, and quick. Because there was nowhere to sleep for the night, and the landscape was bereft of anyone who wanted to meet this changeling version of myself. No one wanted to be my friend.

Freedom. Solitude. The edgelessness of things. I was out in space as wide as places that brag about their wideness, their enormous skies and views without end. And I realized that for all my complaints about feeling hemmed in by family, choices, lack of means, it was far more terrifying to have, literally, no structures at all. I was naked as a pioneer on a land I did not want to possess. I wanted a neon sign to illuminate, a door to swing open, with voices ghosting out like single-malt perfume. I wanted to hug a stranger, lie to his girlfriend, smile till it hurt.

A young man in a bar back home told me half a story about a party he went to in a foreign city. The women, the bookshelves, the way people seemed to be leaning against the air. I excused myself from what I called (to myself) his pretense and wound up on the other end of the bar, playing football with my shot glasses. Now I was desperate to know the end of the story. The names of the women, the authors of the books. I wanted to be at that party, holding my piss to hear the end of any story. The end of everything. That was it. The end. I suddenly could not stand not knowing the end. When I didn't care about my own destruction, I had had no interest in anyone else's. But in this gaping maw of acres, I lusted for any end at all. A punch line. The credits. A simple good night.

Instead I found a church. Or a temple. I couldn't tell the religion, all iconography having been stripped, stolen, and smashed into so many pieces that even God didn't know who was praying to him here. It was white stucco and as unprotected as a teenage girl in the city. Yet, despite missing chunks from the reverberations of a thousand bombs, it was still standing, adorned with a tree in front like an Edenic bodyguard.

I sprinted toward it so quickly that I skidded into the tree, adding a few splinters to my seared hands. The tree was still in bloom, leaves as green as moss, with metal fragments like diamonds in its hair. The branches hung down over the door, tapping at it, as if on my behalf. I didn't need an invitation. I was going in. The door was glued shut by moisture and disuse. I cut along the seal like a murderer returning to the scene of the crime. And with a third linebacker push, it not only opened, it came off its rust-knuckled hinges.

There wasn't enough light to discern anything more than a few toppled chairs, or boxes used as chairs. The final gatherings here had been informal and probably panicked. When they fled they must have realized no one would be coming back. As I walked toward where the altar should have been, I could see it had been taken apart and burned for warmth. Perhaps the locals had believed this was the final safe place in the pockmarked city. They would have been right. They should have stayed. Although the interior was stripped of any identifiers, its lack of windows, especially the stained-glass variety, gave it a casual air. Yes, worship, prayer, collections had taken place here. But never in a hurry, I could tell. It didn't feel like most churches I had been in: a place demanding a rapid escape. The walls were warm to the touch, and I realized the thickness of the foundation and the insulation of the almost adobelike stucco made the building temperate at all times. The stripping of the altar hadn't been for warmth. It had been for fuel.

I fingered through the ashes. Maybe leftovers, even molding, would say where the hell I was. I began to feel giddy and unprepared. My shoulders weakened, and knees. Sleep. That was what was cascading down, like a waterfall within. It was taking me over the rocks of my fatigue, asking for smoothness, waiting to simply lay me down. "I'm not sleeping," I called out, taking help from a plastic chair to keep from falling.

"Hah," I heard my mother say. "All you ever did was sleep in church, honey. Don't you know that's why I stopped bringing you boys? I didn't want people thinking you weren't getting enough rest at home." She laugh-smiled, as if she were both pulling my leg and telling the truth. She looked beautiful and old, standing where the choir should have been singing.

"I must be exhausted," I answered. "If you're here. To tuck me in." I ambled toward her, like a rookie cowboy in new spurs. She caught my fall and laid me down on the cool,

cool floor in one motion. It was as smooth as the surface of God's palm. "Will you be here in the morning?" I asked.

"You know the answer." My mother smiled again. She held my wounded hands as if they weren't wounded at all.

"No. Mom. I don't know the answer to anything."

"Sure, you do," she comforted, crossing my hands across my stomach, looking at me with purity only the invisible possess. "You know who you are. And that's everything."

"What if . . . ?" I began, but she was already gone. I watched her glance off the windowless walls, surf out on a tree branch, and curl up into the ocean-black sky. ". . . It feels like nothing?"

The answer came back just as I lost the battle to stay awake, but I heard it clear as the bells this church had lost. Didn't matter who said it. Me. My mother. Some other hallucination sent to get me through the night. But this answer came with no solace. "Then that's what it is."

Two months and four days after we buried my brother under a headstone so generic I couldn't single it out even as I stood in front of it, I took a job cutting grass. It wasn't about starting a summer business or a desire to get out of the house. Searing myself, as my mother called it, hoping that heat could burn away the gauze that had enshrouded me since the crash.

"You're under there," she would say. "I can see you." Her voice had the thin optimism of a bettor watching his team lose and the clock wind down in double time. And the house I chose to offer my services to, at an exceedingly fair rate, was not chosen for its lawn size or proximity to the neighborhood. When I knocked on the door, there was only one motivation bending my elbow, fisting my fingers. I wanted to see what this family did with the vacancy at their table. Because it was their father, husband, provider, who had left earth the same moment my brother did. Strangers in life, partners at the very moment it ended.

The woman who opened the door was thin on the top and wide on the bottom, as if someone had tried to yank her up and out of herself through the eye of a needle and failed. Her hair was dusted with dark gray, and everything she was wearing was corduroy. Brown pants, tan vest, blue topcoat, all corduroy. She was on her way out and eager to say no. I told her I was new to the neighborhood, strapped for cash, a hard worker, and that her lawn was in need of tending. Only the final piece was true. My tumult of words kept her silent just long enough to change her mind. She gave me a ten-dollar advance and keys to the garage for the mower.

I never spoke to her again. Not because I stole her car and vanished into a cross-country crime spree. But because in my seven weeks of cutting the W.s' grass, I never saw her again. I saw her silhouette through the crooked second-floor curtains. I watched her pull into the garage, post-groceries, and close the door behind her with an exhausted tug. But I later guessed that the only reason she spoke to me at all that first day was shock. She'd turned mute since her husband's death and hadn't opened the door to answer my knock but to exit for a long drive along unknown roads where she could zero out her mind. My knock simply coincided with her escape. So she had to let me in. I'd heard her speak. She'd need me close to ensure I kept the secret.

The couple's youngest son was a shaggy-bearded creature caught between high school and college like a climber who'd fallen through a crevasse. He was still alive, but he knew no one was coming to rescue him. He only spoke to me to try to sell and/or buy drugs. Neither transaction ever went down, but he was relentless in his hopefulness. "That's right," he'd say. "You don't." Then he'd brush bangs from his eyes and lean back as if he were getting high just by talking about it.

On Saturdays, with his mother on a long drive to nowhere, he would sit in a vinyl beach chair with enormous headphones on and watch me circumnavigate the expanse of their lawn. It wasn't until my last day of work that I discovered he was listening to inspirational tapes, not liquid metal. Be better. Be stronger. Be taller. I listened with jaw open until he caught me. Explained that words were the only thing that blocked out the lawn mower noise. I bought it until I guessed he needn't be outside at all. "No AC," he said, guessing my question.

And then I asked for what I'd wanted since the moment I'd walked up their slate path. "Can I come inside?"

I needed to see if the W.s' house felt as blown open as ours did. To see if there was a tear in the roof the size of a man. Wanted to see if it was harder to inhale because all the oxygen had been taken, the living room as cold and useless as a burgled bank vault. The son led me inside, and the heat was like a warning. No AC indeed, but all the windows were shut as well. It was as if they wanted to hang on to whatever dust and self the dead man had left behind. The son led me room to room on an unnarrated tour ending in the kitchen, which is where he assumed I'd wanted to go. "My dad died, so there's no beer," he flat-toned. "I'm not old enough." And then the tears. They ran down his face so fast that they hung on his chin like icicle droplets. He didn't bother to wipe them away. He looked at me, his eyes broken, his chin dimpled and hard with grief. "He was a good guy."

There are some events that nothing prepares you for. Or maybe movies do, or books, lies you hear a friend tell. Things that are so alien to you that to even imagine doing them brings a laugh that sticks in the throat like an unswallowed pill. But then a man-boy weeps in his kitchen without knowing who you are. That you are a spy. That you are investigating the landscape of your own nothingness. And the only possible reaction out of the trillion that the universe offers is what you do. You hug him. You hold him till his tears are hot through your summer-sweated tee. You hold him till he stops shaking, taking the seizure into yourself in the hope of shocking your heart alive. You hold him in silence as his sobs become questions become prayers become silence. And then, when the unrehearsed ritual is over, and that moment is as clear as the decision to embrace . . . you back away like a monk, head down. And never visit there, anywhere near there, ever again.

When I got home that day, my mother grabbed me by the shoulders like a tailor fitting a suit. "You are," she said, "brown as a berry."

"Berries are blue." I smiled. My first smile since. "Sometimes they're straw or ras. But they are never brown."

"This one is." Her forefinger pressing the tip of my nose. We stood in the foyer, dumbfounded by, if not happiness, then a gaping lack of sadness. "Should we . . . ?" she asked, her expression finishing her sentence. On any other day it would have ended, "call your father for dinner?" Or "clear the table, do the dishes?" But this one ended differently. We needed permission from each other, permission to let go of this hypnosis. To return to before. Yet the problem was that our before was so graceless, so faceless, that at least in grief we'd found a small disturbance along the way. An exit ramp. A place to lie low, hide out, and not be whatever we were. "Should we" ended with "return, go back, de-

scend." And it made the grief seem comforting, almost allur-
ing in its foreignness. We both nodded no, not ready to let
go yet. It wasn't for little brother, it was for us. And if his
final gift to us was this grief, then it would be wrong to put
it up on the shelf before we had used up everything it had to
offer.

That was the dream that my mother had tucked me in
with. A good memory from an endless file of unhappy ones.
She veiled me with it, and, when the voice returned, this
time yelling, and closer, I did not want to yield to waking. I
bit my lids down tight as coffins and felt the hot breath of the
exhortation.

"Get up."

Not ready. I yanked myself down deeper into sleep,
deafer as I fell away. Forcing memories to become the dream
of the dream to unpack more memories. I could feel the
muscles of my mind carve and strain at the descent. Up
above, the outline of my alarm clock, barking mute over my
sleeping. He didn't know my sleeping was anything but laziness or rest. It was an energy. A tirade. A defiance that re-
quired all my strength, real and imagined. And then he was
gone. I was back inside.

I began to hover like a bird caught between two winds,
and watched the landscape change below me. Me at ten,
breaking a toy I couldn't figure out how to use, the plastic

leaving a six-inch tear in my flesh as its defense. Me at four-teen, standing outside a school dance with an untorn ticket and a too-tight tie. It was my father's, and it bowed out at the bottom like I was wearing a napkin. Me at six, climbing a tree, hoping to fall, not having the nerve to jump. Almost midnight when my father climbed up to snatch me down, his fingers pressing into me like a trumpeter holding a note. "Happy now?" he'd said to my shivering self.

"Yes," I'd said. Whack.

The memories lazy-Susaned by long enough to enter-tain. It didn't matter that they stung. Just that they'd already happened. Already hurt me. Whatever was awaiting my awakening had the power to hurt me in the now. I didn't seem to have enough strength for new pain. So I lingered on the past. My memories suddenly felt like burning money. I could see their worth only as they disappeared.

Me at seventeen, trying to steal a car by mimicking the hot-wiring I'd seen on cop shows. Wound up laughing so hard at my ineptitude that I drew a cop's attention. "You all right, son?" the wide-nostriled officer asked.

"Lost my keys," I lied.

"Laugh so you don't cry. I get it," he smiled. Then he gave me a lift. When my mother saw the squad car dropping me off, she ran out in worry, concocting an unnecessary alibi as she ran. "Mom, it's cool," I calmed her. "Thinking of joining the force."

"Good kid, ma'am," the officer said, tipping his hat, checking out my mother's figure, the house. He seemed to want to move in.

"My husband agrees," Mom lied.

"I'm sure he does." The cop backed away as if we had the gun and drove off chastened.

"Why'd you do that?" I asked.

"Because I felt like a pie in the window."

"Not such a bad thing."

"Never mind that," she said, backpedaling in her furless slippers. "You're not really wanting to become a policeman."

"Nah," I answered, half disappointed, watching the cruiser turn off of Victory. "Tried to steal a car."

"What?" Without bothering to stop at the door.

"Don't worry. I'm no good at that either."

Me at twenty-four. In the village pub with an unquenchable thirst. Pints of beer disappeared as if they'd been spilled. Not wanting to drink, yet ordering another. Drowning. Ordering another. The rage of it all kept me sober. Girls rotated by like pieces on the game board of my life. Staying only long enough to want to roll the dice, get the hell away. In this dream I felt exactly as I had during the actual experience. I wasn't there. Just above or just outside, my body as artist's replica, my voice useless, my presence an injury. Present, just not accounted for.

I went outside without paying, the sunset like a hood

pulled over bright orange eyes. It was six-thirty, and I was fifteen beers in.

A young couple passed me on their way into the bar. "They got live music?" Both had the forced cheeriness of people who needed to have a good time like an infant needs a vaccine.

"You know where you are?" I asked, the tiniest of slurs.

"Yes."

"Then you should leave."

"Let's go, baby," the girl said, sensing the darkness in me before her blond, sweatered boyfriend.

"I like this town," the guy said. He wanted it competitive.

"Don't you get it, sport?" I spoke to him like an uncle to a child. "Everything entertaining is either happening tomorrow or was on last night."

"He's drunk," girlfriend muttered. "Let's go."

"Run inside, sport. She's right. You won't like how this conversation ends." He wanted to do something bold. To rise up like a primitive and smack my smart ass down. His girlfriend pulled at him, her arms tight as reins.

"I like it here. You don't, you can't just . . ." All I had to do was lean in. That's how scary I was in that unscary environment. He cowered as if hit, his dignity shed like a winter coat. She saw it. She saw how a simple gesture had undressed her man. It would end their relationship. If not that night, then soon after. She hit me. Punched me hard in the arms and chest for stealing him from her. Hit me until the boyfriend was the one pulling her away. My shoulders burned from her small angry fists. It felt, not good, but something.

"You folks have a good night," I said, still not moving from my spot.

"Fuck you," she yelled/swallowed. And they were inside.

"I agree," I said. "I agree completely."

"Soldier!" That was the word that woke me up. That was the word that completed the dream. Being the drunk asshole had gotten me into this position. The dream had become a sober reality. I wanted to fight over nothing just to feel alive, and the hotel had given me that chance. "Soldier!"

"What?" I said, sitting up so fast that I grazed R.'s cheek with my forehead.

"We gotta move."

"How long did I get?" I asked, unfurling to an awkward stance. My feet were so tingled it was like stepping on frozen shards of glass.

"Sorry. Gotta move."

I crab walked to the door and outside saw the exact sky I'd left behind. In the fast approaching distance, the clear sound of truck tires and voices.

R. yelled, "We need a vehicle," as if volume would grant his wish.

"I feel like I didn't sleep at all."

"You didn't, kid. I watched you lie down." So I hadn't been sleeping. I'd been hiding. First refuge of the insane, the waking dream.

"Where were you?" I said as he took off in a walk-run away from the church.

"Behind the vestibule. Came in through the choir door. Listening to you talking to your goddamn mother." I caught up to him, but he wouldn't look at me.

"I met a peacekeeper," I said. "Dutch. Dead."

"Thought you said you met him."

"He died after."

"You kill him?"

Almost, I thought. I'd wanted to in the beginning. "I haven't killed anybody."

"Except Y. Great war, eh, kid? All these enemies and all you killed yourself was a fellow grunt." We reached the top of a small rise where we could see down onto a flooded street, where the water looked neck-deep if it looked an inch. Stopping let us guess how close the trucks were. We had less than a minute. "Water main," R. said, as if explaining it would make it passable. There was no end to the break to the left or the right. And because it was on a slight decline, the water funneled through at speed. Fear fingered around my ribs and brain. I felt electric with terror, that if I touched the water I could have put out the stars.

Closer. The trucks rolled with the certainty of the re-
volving earth. The voices were closer now. The language,
English as broken as the landscape. "It doesn't matter," R. admitted. I wanted it to not, for it to be just another moment
of disappointment, ambivalence, nonchalance, the void. But
I hated being needled to this shimmering edge, like a butterfly awake for the pin.

"There's only jumping. We could get across." R. looked
afraid, too, his body like a package damaged in the shipping.
But we didn't jump. We simply stood at the flood's edge
and watched carcasses drift by. Each body that passed
seemed to have died in the crossing. Bloated and floating,
their arms in midstroke as if they might still make it. The top
half of a deer swooshed by, antlers close enough to grab.
R. did, pulling out a mounted trophy from some hunting-
themed restaurant. We laughed and held it high as if we'd
bagged it.

"I thought for a minute . . ."

"I know, I know," R. said.

"I mean, where the hell are we? A deer. What city is this?"
and I laughed, even shouldered against him, hoping desperate kinship would squeeze out the answer.

"Fucking deer," he said instead.

The trucks were upon us. Vision was useless, but our
ears told us that we'd reached our end. We had waited on
this edge for a reason. Somehow, courage had abandoned us,

but so had panic. It wasn't fight or flight, it was neither. We waited as the convoy approached.

"Better load," R. said. "I guess." He sounded like an old man deciding to get in off the porch for supper. Exhausted, hungry for nothing, yet obliged to behave in some familiar fashion. We hoisted our weapons as the volume played in our ears, bright and insistent as an ice cream truck in July.

"Maybe they can't see us," I wished.

"They can see us."

"Then why can't we see them?"

"Just . . . wait." We splayed out onto the soggy ground, guns like cameras to capture the moment of arrival. The earth smelled like a ruined greenhouse. Dead flowers and stale herbs. Face this close, the soft soil seemed to be sucking us down, a head start on our graves. I squinted against the dissident air as it refused to show us our enemy.

"Come on," I hoarsed. "Hurry up." The trucks, maybe fifteen or twenty of them, were now less than fifty feet away, their speed unabated. The voices were a choir of yelling and distortion. "I know," I recommended. "Let them roll over us into the water."

"Good for the first few. The rest'll figure it out."

"Fuck 'em. If we die, let's take a few with us."

"Who said we're going to die," R. flatlined.

Your voice does, I wanted to say. He already sounded dead.

I saw the grill first. It shone oddly bright as it zoomed out of the fog and into view only ten feet away. It was going fast enough that it wouldn't have had time to brake and miss the water. And it was at an angle to pass us by. We could have remained invisible, at least for another moment. But R. decided to shoot. Stand and shoot. Unload a fusillade like a last stand. World War II soldier, lonely in his foxhole. He screamed as he shot, knowing his death was imminent, and he wanted to go out with nothing left in the barrel. His bellowing drowned out my shouts for him to get down, to save bullets, to do anything but what he was doing. He might as well have lit himself on fire for all the focus he was pulling in our direction.

One of his bullets worked. I saw it crease the windshield and pierce the driver's windpipe. The driver slumped onto the wheel, his body knocked sixty degrees wrong, and the truck began to spin in its own tracks. I stood and throttled R. to the ground, his last bullets puncturing the earth around us in useless thumps. His breathing was heavy, his mouth crooked as a boxer punched. "What the fuck?" I wanted to punish him, adrenaline barbwiring through my veins.

"Shhh," he said, his eyes mad-happy. "I got him."

"They all know where we are."

"So shhh." We listened. The convoy of trucks still as loud, just out of view. Then slightly quieter, as if retreating. Had

R.'s splurge fooled them into backpedaling? No. The trucks again, close as skin, the voices shouting. "They're not firing," R. said.

"That's because they're not as fucking stupid as —"

"No." And this time he looked at me with actual hope in his eyes. "Because they're not there." R. rose. He unpeeled himself from my grip and walked toward the voices, which now seemed to be retreating again. Like a foolish apostle, I followed him. R. reached the truck first. He timed its spinning and jumped up into the cab, pulling the driver off the gas pedal and out onto the ground. I watched him calmly brush away all the glass from the driver's seat and put the thing in park. The trucks were closer than ever now, the shiver of voices screaming in our ears. Until R. reached across the dash and turned off the recording.

The quiet was so absolute that the water at our back sounded like a country brook. R. sat behind the wheel and slowly realized that he was alive. The face of his youth flickered beneath his tattered age.

The door had the decal of the peacekeepers. And the dead driver was wearing the same uniform Dutchman had on in his photograph. "What was he doing?"

"Trying to scare . . . whoever."

"It worked."

"Not for him." We dug a small grave as the night settled in around us. We snapped the antlers off the deer head to make a bone cross. R. looked confused as we stood wordless in front of the grave.

"Don't feel bad," I said. "You . . ."

"Don't try to comfort, bleeder. Soldier shouldn't know how."

"Bullshit" jumped out of my mouth.

"I don't feel . . . anything but alive."

"What if this is it?" I asked. "What if there isn't even a war anymore? Just assholes driving in circles to scare assholes who are running in circles?" R. didn't have time to answer. The explosion tore the night into a Halloween party of black and orange and catapulted us into the surging water. I surfaced first, then R., then the deer head without its antlers, floating on in its wonderment, staring up at the bright dark. R. and I both thought about speaking but then took the deer's approach. Lay on our backs and decided to see where the flood wanted to take us.

We floated, the emasculated deer head, R., and I. Floated like apples waiting to be bobbed for by competing angels. The water was filthy and deeper than the ocean had seemed. The speed of the current allowed me to be flat on my back and fear neither sinking nor arrival. Whatever part of the city we were passing was submerged to the point of invisibility. The only hint of injury from the blast was a creeping sting from shin to thigh. I could feel with my fingers that my fatigues had been split, but no shrapnel was protruding. And this had been the good leg, the one that hadn't been chopsticked by the land mine. The enemy was taking the theory of limb-by-limb very seriously.

Crunching up, I could see R. about five feet to my left. He was making swimming motions as if a coach were watching him. Useless but perfectly executed. So I decided to simply lie back until we got beached.

The night sky was lifting its hem, teasing at the day that lay behind. And directly overhead, close enough to shoot, appeared a hawk. The first living nonhuman creature I'd seen since exiting the hotel. It was still too dark to call its color, but it flew in a straight line on wings of authority. And it traveled equal to the current's speed. If the water pocketing into my ears didn't remind me I was moving in haste, it would have seemed motionless, as if nailed to the wall of sky.

The underbelly had two tones, and the tail was split into three sections that shimmered and beat in the air like a summer girl's hair. My ex-wife's hair, long as July, striped by air and sun as she walked faster than I, like she always did. Perpetually in a rush to beat me anywhere. See a thing first. Register surprise, then pass the story on to me. For a while, when love was still bright-white as an inhalant, I stopped looking at things. Only wanted to hear them described. Listen to her apricot voice grant shape to a painting, a landscape, or a building, more vibrant in her tone than any architect could draw. We once did a walking tour of a historical site without my ever opening my eyes. "Everyone thinks you're blind," she laughed, pulling me toward another landmark.

"I am."

She spoke with the certainty of facts despite her lack of education. She knew the essence of what had gone on there, and her imagination must have made history jealous. The silver teeth of bayonets and smoking failure of muskets. Men booted in mud, waiting to be stolen from life. Cannons drumming in jazz rhythm. One, two, three, four, boom, one, boom, wo ta ra ra boom deeay. And then she'd be singing. Pulling my blind self into a dance, into a wrestle, into a heap of laughter that bordered on a seizure.

She was the first and last to make me laugh like that. As if she had a coin that operated the mechanism of happy. And once I sent her away, they stopped making that coin. Or my works rusted over from lack of use.

That was her magic. To take the ancient pain of the land and spin it into laughter from a sullen boy. I needed her now, now that I was the ruined soldier, ducking bullets and sinking into the mud. History wasn't stories, or even survival. History was death piled on top of death until the earth crashed into the sky.

The hawk was lower. Or the water was higher, but history was happening, and I was the one caught in between.

"R.," I shouted, sitting up, not yet ready to be crushed.

No answer. The deer head took its last gulp and sank. R. wasn't where he had been. Maybe his strokes had pulled him ashore. I began to mimic the same. Freestyle, freestyle, I reminded myself. Breaststroke too slow, backstroke too perpendicular, butterfly too fucking hard. Freestyle. The water tasted of iron and wine. I suddenly wanted to tilt the world and drink the battlefield dry. One gulp told me that wasn't the solution to finding my leader. I gagged out the drown like a child on ipecac.

Suddenly getting out of this flow was more important than breathing. I needed a hard surface. R.'s bitter eye (the one good one) laughing at me as I crawled out of the muck. Or the dead gleam of an overturned truck with the seats torn out. A fort. A pile of sand. Anything not wet.

I threw a sideways glance and there the hawk hung, its wings as open as church doors. "Point me," I spit at my hawk. And then I trusted. With each stroke I felt stronger. The sting in my leg had subsided to a dial tone, and my arms felt exactly as powerful as they were. Stroke, another, third one brought my face out of the water. Find the hawk. Follow the hawk. There he was. Good. Swim.

I was going so fast that my last pull with my right shoulder plugged my arm into wet earth up to the elbow and skidded me to a halt. Water tugged at my waist, but I was able to left-hand my body forward inch by inch until I was up onto a tiny rise and out of the flood. I breathed as quietly as I could, waiting, waiting to hear R. lambaste me. Nothing. I pivoted like a mermaid, torso only, the pain in my leg surfacing like tiny, jagged flowers. All thorn, no rose. The hawk was gone, too. I scanned the sky, a child who'd lost his kite. "Shit," I said. Lovely, I thought. Everyone keeps leaving.

Then, suddenly, the bird, quiet as sleep, was perched on my leg. He stood just below the wound, my exposed ankle as perch. "Where's R.?" I asked the hawk, fully expecting an answer.

His response hurt like hell.

Beak into flesh, the hawk hammered down into my wound. And only into my wound. Again. Again. Blood splashed out in miniature waves, wine spilled from a glass. Again. The pain was spectral, diamonds of sweat jumping from my pores. It was as if I was being disassembled one nerve at a time. The hawk paused every six or seven attacks, looking at me as if to reassure himself I wasn't going to reach down and strangle him, which I was close enough to do, or claim my leg back. He sensed I'd given it to him, the way I'd trusted his navigation.

I saw a painting in my mind, bright and bold as the moment my ex had described it to me. We were in a museum, and I was blind again to enjoy her description. The painting was of a man, chained by circumstance, wearing little but his helpless scowl and a beard she described as "important." And yet this man with the important beard was being attacked by a cruel creature. A bird who tore into his flesh with razored precision and sought to pull from him whatever hid beneath the skin.

"Why are you telling me this?" I complained, eyes squeezed tight.

"Because it's true."

My hawk dipped in again, then paused. Though I was still, the earth trembled around me, as if to frighten off the bird I had failed to dismiss. His beak and face were chocolaty with blood as he opened his mouth and dropped a tiny glowing pellet. It played melon green against the hard night background. And the pellet joined more than thirty others, still phosphorescent, on the ground. The hawk surveyed my injury again, shopping for another pellet but not digging in. The wound now clean of the metal tracers the bomb had injected me with, my hawk flew away. Circling. Keeping an eye until the air erased him from the page of night.

I pushed myself away from the water and the shrapnel as if both might jump back into my leg and finish the job. "Mc. would have liked that story," I said out loud. "He would have known it was true." But there was no reply. No R. over my shoulder like the bad guy in a movie. No hallucination of my ex spreading a picnic blanket, telling me an olive was a blueberry when she popped it into my mouth. Then laughing when I spit it out because it's not how a thing feels, it's what we expect it to feel like. No. Nothing. No partner to lie down with. Only the angry gape of my leg to remind me where I was. Or that I was even alive. "A fuckin' hawk," I laugh-shouted into the air.

And then there were arms under me, no, through me, through the space between my pits and my ribs. Strong arms yanking me backward at rescue velocity. The sky had lit up again with sulfur scores and wasted flame painting corners of the morning canvas. Tracers whizzed by my feet and face. Heat from an explosion passed over us hot as August. I was thinking *us* without knowing who my other half was. I was being dragged too rapidly to turn back and identify him. And the noise from the largest firefight I'd encountered since leaving the hotel made conversation moot. Whoever it was cared more for my safety than his own, willing to be target for so long just to hump my wounded self to possible safety.

"Soldier. The leg." His voice finally threaded through the space between dimensions. "Can it go?" For a flash, I thought he was suggesting amputation.

"It goes," I shouted, trying to bend it to show off dexterity. Had it curled up, almost boot to butt, when he let me go.

"Follow," he spat, and I was up. Tearing after this fatigued hero toward a cinder-block building, rather, a pile of cinder blocks, nearly fifty yards away. I was stunned at how much I could see. The landscape was its brightest, morning plus bombs making for a generous display of light. And the hits were coming from three directions. Rocket launchers, mortar rounds, the invisible slash of old-school machine-gun bullets, all raining the air in a constant assault of triangles.

"Who's firing?" I yelled, but hero was ahead, gesturing like a man late for a train. I didn't want to be in this stranger's control. Even if it was toward safety. I wasn't ready to be carried, even though I needed it. Should've opened my eyes by the water's edge, I thought, my mouth open in lifeless retreat. Should've played dead.

Like hero did. In front of me. Only he wasn't playing. Bullets like bees stung him into a circle. He pirouetted once, then knees, then face into the ground. I pulled him out of the muck, his mouth a soup of blood and earth. Did my best arm hoist and began pulling him toward the cinder blocks. My back burned like my flesh was being tightened. But he had pulled me at least this far. I was going to make it, to see what was so goddamn great about these cinder blocks. What made them worth dying to see.

The road became bumpy. Seemed a lot of soldiers had spent their final moments scrambling for the cinder blocks. My path became a slalom between bodies posed like statues. Unbronzed. Unremembered. I heard a corpse's ribs crack like peanut shells as I sought footing over a small berm.

I slipped in oil from a former truck, its naked frame making it look let down by the rest of the assembly line. The oil seeped into my shirt, cheap perfume, but I never lost stride. Hero was getting where these other slow-foots hadn't. Even if it was going to be his grave. I needed to be in that truck, not just dragging past it. I needed the revolution of wheels, a motion I had always taken for granted. Like a teenager in a fifties beach flick, I needed wheels. Or something even simpler. A wheelbarrow.

We had a wheelbarrow in our garage growing up, the hell for. But it did spend one summer as little brother's and my favorite mode of transportation. At ten I was too young and short to even attempt to steal dad's car, and at five my bro fit so ideally inside the damn barrow, it seemed to have been custom built for the little guy's transport action.

I took him on races up and down Victory, versus invisible foes to guarantee a win. "Another victory on Victory," I'd celebrate. And his arms would shoot up like tiny goal posts.

"Victawy!" (Someone should bottle how a little kid talks. Save the world.)

We wheeled down to the corner after the ice cream truck had passed in front of our house. We liked to see if we could reach the last stop sign before he turned right and gone. If we didn't make it, we figured we didn't deserve the treat. Twice we raced it down the front stairs inside the house. First time brother went flying into the coatrack, saved only by Dad's bearskin jacket and ridiculous matching hat. Softest thing our father ever did for either of us. Second time, it left wheel prints in a perfect mud-strip pattern down the seventeen beige carpet stairs. "We could say it's new," I offered to my mom. And for a moment, impossibly, she seemed to be entertaining the idea. Then the car in the driveway, and soon the carpet wasn't the only part of the house with a new imprint on it.

I managed to hide that the wheelbarrow was the culprit (a bike was blamed, and quickly interred), and this prolonged the summer of rickshaw-esque joy. We used it so often, my mother became worried about her youngest losing his ability to walk. So we showed her that he could push me as well. About three feet, but still. Next thing, Mom's in the barrow with two sons serpentining her down the backyard slope like drunk coal miners late with a delivery.

I needed a wheelbarrow that day. I needed to be pushing hero, not pulling him. I could have navigated us to any destination with grace and wily speed. Known when to duck, to swerve, to screech to a halt, only to roll on again. But yanking him backward, blind in all but one foot, and this destination promising only because he was rushing me this way. What if there wasn't even a nook to hide behind? What if the enemy had already taken it? Who the fuck was the enemy? So I stopped. In protest of not understanding anything at all, I stopped. The bullets did not. I dropped down beside my clearly deceased hero and used him as one hundred

ninety pounds of blockade. He looked like me, only a few
battles older. Even in death, his face seemed tense. Lived.
Scars railroaded across his chin, lips, and cheek. He was
American. Standard issue uniform, top to bottom, though
roughnecked by the proceedings. I managed to open his
rucksack, take ammo and his sidearm. Last bit of water I
used for a quick swig, then to wash the blood and mud off
his face.

"Thank you." I said it, but it felt like it was coming from
him, too. Such minuscule tenderness, always too late, was a
comfort in the knowing and the doing.

A bullet tore into his dead legs, stopping an inch short of
mine. I could see the nub of the slug nosing out of his pants.
As far as protection, the cinder blocks had to be better than
this. I placed my hand on his chest as good-bye and leverage,
then low-sprinted as fast as I could. The blocks were only
twenty feet away, and I dared to believe that I deserved at
least that much. If I had succeeded in not dying yet, then
reaching this arbitrary yet necessary way station somehow
seemed fair. When survival seemed impossible, nothing surprised me. But this close to being able to hide was a tease. So
I dreamed myself bulletproof until the cinder blocks could
make it so.

I hugged the first block so hard as I swung around behind
it that I took a layer of skin off my face. And it felt good. I

smiled. Looked around to find someone to show it to. The white of my teeth. The fresh aliveness of my injuries. Look at me. I'm a soldier.

But no one had made it that far. I was alone. And I suddenly realized that all the dead around me hadn't been miming toward this construction. They'd been sprinting away from it. The bars that had separated the cells now lay as splayed and crooked as old car parts. The bomb that tore open this prison at the impact point was now molecularized into the metal-hard dirt.

There were a few odd survivors. A porcelain toilet bowl, sideways but proudly intact. Half a sink, looking like the faucet had frozen in middrip. But it was only the stretched metal of the melted faucet itself. One wall was nearly unmarked, with chains and hoops and makings that indicated this was the torture chamber. Of course, the one thing to outlive all is the means of torture. In the end it'll just be two big guns aimed at each other, dreaming of a living thing able to pull the trigger.

The triangle of attack had slowed enough that I could try to do a little inventory. My leg wound was still wide as a child's shovel and raw to the sight. But it hurt far more when I looked at it than when I didn't. It was going to live. I did a routine bone check, as they'd taught us at the hotel. Adrenaline was a great masker of pain, and men had been known to be running on a fracture until the bone interrupted the skin like a white exclamation point. Nothing broken. All joints operable. I checked hero's handgun. Loaded. My hands were quivering, but I willed them to stop. For the first time since I'd lain down in the church, a sense of calm visited, even as the fighting stirred beyond my prison.

Were these military prisoners? Was this a holiday pen for civilian suspects awaiting trial? In a war-torn country, anything was possible. Shoplifters would get tortured under the right regime. So there was no way of knowing who had been incarcerated without crawling back into the crossfire and examining who had died fleeing the coop. Not. Quite. Yet. I was enjoying, nearly luxuriating in the privacy of these two and a half walls. The crater invited a deeper sense of protection. But all because, once I reached the jail, not a single round came anywhere near me. No wonder hero had been racing us here. Perhaps he'd been encouraged, safe and waiting, when he binoculared a fellow grunt pulling himself up onto the unannounced beach. And, as heroes do, he ran and grabbed me with only one oath in mind. I couldn't say I was feeling similarly inspired. I had had my fill of looking. It was a relief not to be checking every angle for possible demons and daredevils, snipers and fiends. I needed sleep. The sleep R. had stolen from me at the church. I did make a pact with myself that, exhausted or not, an R. sighting would prompt a hurried rescue, or at least a signal to make a run for this concrete haven. But with my eyes dropping like bank windows, seeing anything but black seemed remote.

Extreme fatigue is like an illness. It steals the limbs first, like frost climbing up a lawn deer. Then, the heart, so slow it feels packed in gauze and encircled by closed chambers, asleep in its own bed. The mind goes somewhere in between. Static. Clarity. Tears. Terror. Peace. In the moments before unconsciousness, there is only gratitude and anger, fleshed together, antitwins. And then, in a white flash of slumber, everything is, no, everything *seems* OK.

In my dream, the dead prisoners surrounded me like buddies at a poker game. They explained where they were from, how tall they were in high school, what had led them to this visible end. They were of every ethnicity and bore no markings of the damage death had pounded into them. Ranging in age from twenty to fifty, in demeanor from sullen to self-righteous. Their uniforms were neat, with only the identifying flags torn off the shoulders. As if dying was a disgrace to their country.

"No country dishonors their dead soldiers." I complained to them. My voice felt trapped and gummy, like a sparrow on a tar roof.

"This is no country."

I had a thousand questions to ask, but there was no time between their memories. They overlapped each other's stories, looming from one to the next with the thinnest strands of color as a bridge. But they held. What language were they speaking? Was it mine, or me understanding theirs? Were they even using words at all? Yet I seemed to know the ending of almost every tale: Money lost down the sewer? The smallest dog in the neighborhood lowered down with tape on his paws. Cut from the freshman basketball team? Needed to get a job, couldn't honor the time commitment, make all the practices. Liar. Scrape on the neck from a father's too-rough punishment? Ran into a clothesline in the dark.

Even in the dream, I put my hand to my throat.

The men's faces had something else in common. They were all listening intently. To their own stories and to each other's, like orchestra members reading unseen sheet music. There was a rhythm to their entries and exits. Not a word was accidental, not a gesture unnecessary. And then, without warning, each began to tell his neighbor's stories. The amber-haired square-jaw with at least forty years lived told the memory of the twenty-year-old boy-man with hair as long and thin as spools of floss. As the older man spoke, he watched twenty to make sure he was getting the story right, waiting for the approving nod, which gently came.

Then a man with a nose that honored his head began repeating the words of the stallion-faced thirty-year-old across from him. He did it with the rigid assurance of a trial witness. But the story was intact, and the orchestra continued. They were all playing different instruments now, but the music of the remembrance seemed to vibrate even deeper once they had taken on each other's fables. They were now caretakers more than orators. Poets. Beseechers. They held the new stories in the cradles of their tongues and raised the sentences up until they were full-grown. Alert. Alive.

When they had finished this gifting, their mouths closed. Then their eyes. Finally, their hands, folded onto their laps. They had accomplished their task. They were silently, reverently waiting for me. To tell them everything I'd heard. To let them furl into whatever's next now that they knew their stories were all vouchsafed with me.

I tried to signal them that they were mistaken. That I could only recall their courage and the familiarity, but not the words themselves. I could never be trusted to share a syllable of all their victories. Their yearning, waiting, their inbetweenness. "Wait," I yelled, my voice still weak, then weaker, "I can't remember . . . all of this." They opened their eyes. "Any of it," I continued, hoping my face would say the rest. Doubt, worry, apology. Need.

"You were the one," twenty said, "who wanted to meet us." No, I thought. I never wanted to know any of this. I hated my own stories. Why would I want to collect theirs?

"These aren't our stories," a new man in the circle said. It was hero, a bullet hole clean through his cheek. "These are yours."

Wake up. Wake up! Asshole, wake up! I said it loud enough to make my circle disappear. They receded or vanished or dusted, each in his own way. But I was still asleep. I could not wake myself, despite being terrified of the circle speakers returning, and this time disappearing me off with them.

"Wake up. Wake up! Asshole, wake up!" Mc. stood over me. His hair copper against the filthy white sky. Bombs popped like corn around us. "Next one's got our name on it" — his laugh making it sound like sticking around for it might be fun. And then he said my name. "Come on. Grab on." He lifted me up, taking my weight. I was still too stunned to deny his energy. Trying to remember where I'd put hero's gun.

"Looking for this?" he said, showing me the weapon, tucking it into his waistband. "I've got it, kid. Looks like they were right. You are a bleeder." He guided me to the edge of the cinder blocks. Beyond it seemed certain death. "Don't be afraid," he said, his voice as smooth as birthday-cake icing. "I'm faster than I look."

Confinement. I suddenly felt so trapped by circumstance and lack of mobility that protest was not something I could articulate. This was beyond what I'd felt when hero was pulling me. This was a sense of permanent yielding. Surrender. I was a hostage. To the war, my ignorance, my injuries, and now to Mc. As he led me, my feet moved as if up the gallows steps. I anticipated a constriction around my neck and heart. The walls of myself were pressing in, pinching organs into useless bags, out of blood, out of oxygen. I wanted to ask him to kill me right there, in the field. I hadn't the strength for a long drag across the vicious landscape. I needed a bullet now. Here, between the eyes, I almost said. If I'd had the strength, I would have found my gun and done it for him.

I have never been successful at anticipating events. Nor at simply waiting for what's next. I've always carried with me the egg of anxiety, fragile, showing cracks at the slightest hint of the unknown. I recall as a boy being nervous whether the diner would have what I wanted to order or if I'd have to pick a new meal all over again. Crack. I was in a perpetual state of predisappointment, self-aborted hope. They won't choose me, she won't like me. This day will never end. This day went by too fast. Over time it had hardened into a violence. To protect myself from these uninvited responses to the simplest events, I chose to create my own responses even before there was anything to respond to. I was eager to fight before being brushed up against in the street. I was ready to mock before someone sounded smarter than I knew I could ever be. I locked all my doors and windows before anyone dared to knock.

Accepting my place in the hotel had been the perfect merging of panic and attack. I could prepare myself for attack because it was almost guaranteed to arrive. Being frightened wasn't a possibility because I was in a constant state of high alert. This war, I had told myself, was going to allow me to finally be who I was without apology, regret, or sadness. It wouldn't cost me my dignity. It would give it to me. That had been the plan.

But, like I said, I was shit at predicting. The war hadn't done anything but remind me of what I lacked. Who I had failed to become. And it didn't offer dying as a heroic so-lution. It showed death as it actually was. Violent. Bloody. Lonely. Wrong. It wasn't the natural end of things, it was the unnatural interruption. This wasn't doing anything but stacking bodies like wood.

"Where are we going?" I finally managed.

"Said," he spoke, "hotel."

"Hotel's gone, Mc." He didn't turn to me, just tugged me onward. "Blown up. Gone." His red hair had turned black and brown from all the ash in the air. His face was sur-real with so many colors he looked like an Indian from the losing tribe. "Tell me, it doesn't matter," I said. "Just tell me where you're taking me, because I'd rather die here." Mc. looked at me even as we picked up speed. Surveyed me with the eyes of a doctor in a hurry for a round of golf.

"Getting us inside."

"There is no inside," I reminded him. "And you sound different. Where are your stories?"

"Nothing funny to tell."

"Sure there is, Mc. Tell the one about how you did it. How you blew up the hotel." Talking was giving me energy. I was climbing out of the hole in my head, could see the edge of my strength again. I didn't have to go anywhere with him.

Mc. didn't answer my accusation. He just tightened his grip on my arm and sped up. I slowed my stride, so that continuing to pull me would cost him. Wanted to wear him down a bit before I took his ass.

"You didn't kill everybody," I bragged. "R. got out, too. Knew where to hide."

"Where's R. now?" he asked, still not defending himself.

"Out here. Alive."

"You don't sound too certain."

"He's alive. He survived you, a traitor playing sick, playing friend. How the fuck . . . ?" Mc. wrapped his opposite hand around my head and covered my mouth. And still we were walking. He had the strength of both of us, as if keeping me close was just a way to drain me dry. Weakness volted through my knees and he caught my extra weight without a flinch.

"I don't know what R. told you. Don't care. I'm just needing you to shut it down now. You're pretty wounded up, so I'll say it's that and stay friends. Because I am out here trying to save your skin at the fucking moment and I do not need your theories, your threats." A rush of trust veined from head to heart to legs. It was the power he'd had over all of us when he'd first arrived.

Fuck him, I thought. Don't let him in. Don't buy the voodoo. He's a soldier and a liar, not a friend. Reach for your gun. Let him carry your weight and reach for your gun. He was looking at me as we marched forward, his hand still firm across my lips. His eyes had the relaxed aggression of a teacher who knows the student has already given in. I let him believe that. I relaxed deeper into his arms, heavy as I could be. My right arm dangled down almost low enough to touch the ground. I felt the brush of knuckled earth and guessed how long it would take to bring my hand to waistband, pull out gun. I practiced it in my mind over and over, until the motion seemed smooth. I had become as awkward to carry as a ten-year-old in from the car. Mc.'s pace had flagged and his breath came to him in late deliveries. Lift, pull, fire, I incanted. No more waiting. One. Two. Three. Bang.

The gun went off. My finger on the trigger. "Asshole!" Mc. shouted as we both fell to the dirt. His hand was on my wrist, where he'd caught me just as I'd lifted the gun to the target. The bullet had missed him by little enough that the very edge of his uniform, by the shoulder, had burned gray in the pass-by. He punched me twice in the face, reflex and relief in each blow. Blood flavored my mouth. "See what you've done?" he shouted, shaking his punching hand like it was broken. "Goddamn it. Open your eyes and see."

Took a minute for the tracers to leave my vision, the electric shock of the claws buzzing across my eyes like tiny white birds. Wiped my nose, unbroken, tasted my blood. Then, finally, I could peel my eyes all the way.

The hotel. Standing alive on a street where all else was flattened and rubbled. Mc. released my hand, and I sat up. We both stared at the hotel, I stunned, he confused and pissed. "Where did you get the idea?" he exhaled.

"Who are we?" I asked him. When he didn't answer immediately, I put the gun to the side of his head. It fit into the tiny indentation just above his cheekbone. Like they had come as a set. Butt and temple. "Who are we, Mc.? What are we doing here?"

"Come inside." His boyishness was returning. He was the kind of man who had *courage* printed on one side, *coward* on the other.

"Inside? I don't even believe it's there. I stood in the basement," I lectured. "I saw the bodies. The money. The safe."

"What money?" Mc. tried to turn to me but only poked his own eye with my gun.

"If somebody doesn't tell me . . . something. I will do it just for fun." My neck veins rose out like runners on a sled.

"There's no one else. Just us. All I know is . . ."

"What?"

"All I know is . . . don't shoot me." Tears and sweat mixed salt as they crisscrossed down his face.

That was enough of a plea. Even better than an answer, which could have easily been a lie. I eased the gun back a few inches.

"Let's go in then," I said, gesturing him to stand, with the pistol as pointer. Took him a while to rotate to all fours, then push up to his feet, like falling in reverse.

"I was trying to save you," he complained, walking toward the hotel five steps ahead.

"We'll see if you were," I answered. "See if you did."

"You were going to shoot me, weren't you? Because you thought this was a mirage?"

"No," I said. "I thought *you* were a mirage." Not a sound now, not even our footsteps as we neared the fancy-doored entrance. My head felt full of water, like I was drowning in plain air.

"What if he's here?" Mc. asked. "Waiting for us." He meant R. or maybe someone else, his boss, since I still believed him a traitor.

"I don't care who's here," I barked, catching up to him, sticking the gun between his shoulder blades, desperate to prove he was real. "I just want to know if we're here." He stopped, the muzzle pressing into him harder.

"What do you want me to do? Knock?" He turned then, that same wicked, crooked pulled-off-another-one smile on his face. I wanted to sledgehammer his teeth like drywall. What is it makes a man love and hate on such a tight pivot? He opened the door without looking away from me. The cool air rushed at us like a loud whisper. "Come on in," he invited. "I hear it's nice, except for the staff." He tugged at my sleeve and I let him guide me inside, leaving the door open behind.

It was the hotel. Just as I had originally left it. Unbombed. Unmarked. It almost felt like coming home.

He shut the door. It sealed like a vacuum and we stood in the lobby. The registration-desk sign still dared to gleam gold.

"This ain't the same place, if that's your worry." Mc. laughed. As if getting a joke late was the only way to understand it fully. "No wonder you thought . . ." and more laughter as he drifted behind the reception desk, scrounged for keys.

I aimed the gun again, this time both hands vising it still. Should I do it slow, I wondered, or just one to the third eye, his punishment as sudden as his appearance?

"You want a suite?" he asked, without looking up. "I think the sevens and nines are suites." He raised his head, a set of keys in each hand. His expression said he knew this time I wouldn't miss. "Kid."

"Shut up."

"Don't shoot the fucking piano player."

"Five seconds."

"The city's got more of these. It's a chain. A goddamn hotel chain. Have you never heard . . . ?" I stepped closer, my hands beginning to quiver, as if the gun were trying to wriggle its way free. "We used them as barracks when this thing started because we thought the enemy'd bomb civilians last," he rushed. And then, instead of retreating, he began to walk toward me. "It was camouflage," he said, the word sounding exactly like what it meant. Obfuscation remained the military's finest skill.

"You blew the first one up."

"No," he said, now in front of the desk, the keys between his fingers like tiny knives. I took a step closer to him, ready to uncamouflage his empty heart. "That came from the sky."

"Why didn't you die?" So I could do it, I thought. He belonged to me. From first moments of friendship to last breath as my enemy.

"Luck," he said.

"Sorry," I spat. "Don't believe in luck."

"It wasn't yours to believe in." He paused, one foot on tiptoe. He was close enough to launch at me. The gun felt too light. I was afraid to crack the handle. Afraid. "I'm your CO. R. went to look for you, so did I. To bring you in." And now his voice was narcotic. Everything seemed to be floating up and away from me, as if I were the only thing in the lobby not suffused with helium. "You need sleep," he explained.

"If they bombed the other, then we're not safe here either." I didn't realize how near he was until he lowered the gun and my arms like he was voting in an election booth. And he had won.

"Safer than outside," he said. "At least for a rest. Sleep is the one thing, soldier, that we can't outrun." He opened one of my palms and pressed a room key in it. "I'll knock in an hour. If nothing falls on us before." And then he was up the steps, two at a time. A man in a hurry to pause.

I don't know how long I stood there. Maybe the entire hour. I studied the details of the lobby, and it did seem the furniture had a little more mileage on it than I recalled. And the arrow pointing to the bar seemed both blacker and thinner than memory allowed.

A second hotel. A chain. It didn't seem impossible. But I hated that Mc. may have been telling the truth. He kept yoyoing from vanguard to villain, and I was beginning to wonder if he was even there at all. I rotated three hundred sixty degrees. I was alone. The stairs had swallowed Mc.'s exit. I held a gun and a key, while the relentlessness of sleep ripped at the periphery. I wasn't quite ready to take it all lying down.

Like spilled mercury, I ran down the stairs. Racing for the subbasement, the one with the blown-open safe. I needed to see that something was real. If this was another army barracks, then it would also have a safe, one with money and maybe a cache of weapons or ammo. Perhaps I could collect enough supplies to exist on the outside. Because if Mc. was right, then this building was more target than haven, and an hour nap could easily drift into a final rest. Down, down, level after level I hustled. It was lower than I remembered, it seemed impossible. The distance so unfamiliar. Maybe he wants me down here, I thought. Easier place to leave my body. He took me here and even now was upstairs plotting . . . waiting.

Paranoia is like a friend who keeps agreeing with you, which is a problem when you don't know what the hell you are saying. Down. One final flight. This looked right. I wound through the empty offices, the gray corridors, like wandering inside a tomb. At the far end was the office I was seeking. I pushed in and found a safe. It was closed but not locked. I opened it quickly, not even certain what I'd hoped to find. What I found made me stop hoping at all. "Mc.!" I yelled as if my voice could travel through five floors of concrete. I needed a friend at this moment, even if he was my enemy.

"Mc.!" I opened the map and spread it out on the floor. It was of a city. It showed the water's edge. The north and south, the shape comforting in its familiarity. "Mc.!" There were no street names or landmarks. Just a series of numbers, strategic markings for a battle. And at the bottom left was a black star over the stamped image of a hotel. *The* hotel.

"Mc.!" This was it. Where we were. Not the name of the city, of course. Not even the country. But it showed where we were, so it just might point the way out. My hands trembled to the brink of tearing the paper. I smoothed it out again and again, every wrinkle feeling like bad directions. There was nothing south of the hotel on the map. So that was either the end of the land or the only safe passage. "Mc.!" I said one more time. Proud and hopeful all at once. Too soon.

"You shouldn't be down here," he said, disappointed and mean, his pistol falling like a pinion while he was still talking. "You really should've just gone to bed." Blackout.

In a vehicle, then. First vehicle I had seen mobile, aside from the peacekeepers' truck. I was in the passenger seat, buckled in, the pain in my head like Monday after a weekend of shouldn't-haves. My sore temple banged against the window in rhythm with the wreckage we were driving over. I opened my eyes enough to see the hard green plastic of the dashboard, the blood and grime on the windshield. I didn't want the driver, whoever he was, to know I was conscious. See more playing dead than you ever do alive. Out the side window, the unlandscape was gray as x-rayed bone. A man-made desert with undetonated missiles for cactuses. I guess that made us the lizards. The only things stupid enough to survive.

Things must be removed for beauty to be revealed. It was a phrase that had been running through my head since I'd stepped out of the hotel that first day. The landscape had a strip-searched knobbiness to it, all knees and elbows, the world bent over and examined until raw. "Things must be removed for beauty to be revealed." The man who had said that to me was a high-school friend's father. A burly man in need of some bodily removal himself. He wore a beard like a mask and breathed heavily, as if he were continually walking up steps. He had said this phrase to my friend and me while we were hand-stripping the paint off his weary colonial at the end of our street. His tone made it seem like we were restoring the Sistine Chapel. As if beneath the twelve layers of egg-nog-yellow and rot-brown paint lay a home of such particular splendor that we would need to shield our eyes when the job was done. The father stood in the driveway, cooking like a sausage in the summer sizzle, watching my friend and me monkey into every crevice with our scrapers and teenage agility.

When the father went inside to rebeer, I quickly asked my friend if any beauty had been revealed. "My old man's full of shit," he said. "But he pays ten an hour."

I'd met O. my junior year in high school. He was the first kid in our grade able to grow a mustache or sprout whiskers of any kind. The fact that he was losing his hair seemed a small price to pay at sixteen. His goatee looked fucking cool. It also got him easy access at the liquor store. We lived in an eighteen-and-over state, and O. looked at least twenty-one. He was tall and awkward as a mantis, without any of the praying. He smoked pot before school, at lunch, and first thing when he got home. It gave him the permanent aroma of burning rubber. O. was the first contemporary who seemed to be moving at the same speed I was. He didn't like his dad, but he had to listen to him. He thought his mom was "cool," though she mostly seemed to be away visiting relatives whenever I was over. I saw her picture a few times in his home, and she seemed way too pretty to be a mom in our neighborhood. Maybe she'd upgraded and O. was too disappointed to tell me. There were two younger sisters who were trespassing into their teen years about a year and a half early. And there was a dog with long ears and an irresistible belly when it came to scratching and wrestling.

From the start, I didn't trust how at ease I felt around O. Our friendship had the creeping impatience of a film you know is going to end badly. The parts didn't add up. Something was going to come up knives when all the pieces were explained. It was the feeling Mc. had elicited in me our first days at the hotel. Too funny. Too at peace with who he is. That's not what it feels like to be alive. The center will not hold.

The summer after our junior year was spent "revealing the beauty" of his father's house and then concealing it quickly with coat after coat of a color called peacock plum. The mom had picked it out, apparently from a swatch. Clearly that had been what peacock plum had been meant to cover. Only a swatch. Writ large across an expansive house, it became the neighborhood bruise. O.'s little sisters were so embarrassed they began spending most of their time at other girls' houses. O.'s father simply stood in the driveway when we descended our ladders for the last time and said, "You boys sure did it." It was both an accusation and a thank-you, so we took our cash and headed for the minimart.

With the task complete, O. decided it was time to teach me how to get high. He had an elaborate system and the enthusiasm of a high-school wrestling coach, but no matter how hard I tried, or how deeply I relaxed, I could not get the proper balance between inhalation and exultation. Never got hungry. Never got happy. Never got high. It was oddly humiliating to fail at something so fundamental. It made me want to rob a store or try heroin. Something legitimately wicked. "You're too you," O. explained. It was as if I had a birth defect and no amount of training could correct it.

"What does that mean?" I asked, wanting to punch something. Hard.

"You know." He was right. I was clanging around in my head too much, performing, playing me, to be able to relax and experience something new. I wanted to control what getting high felt like and therefore could never get there. Not that it was a long-lasting tragedy. I knew four beers would get me as chilled as O. got with a joint. And I didn't even enjoy how that made me feel. I was stuck being too much me, and there was a sick delight in feeling that unreachable.

It could be said, from a distance, that O. was my best friend at the time. Perhaps the best friend I ever had. He asked nothing of me. Never competed against me. We were as good quiet together as we were laughing. Or him high and laughing and me nodding to a song I heard in my head. When he slept with a girl I had mentioned to him once, he apologized. He was nice to his sisters, even when they were mean for no reason, the way only young girls can be. "Hey, baldie!" they would shout if he wasn't giving them what they wanted. "Baldie O'Balderson."

"That's a good one," he'd say to me, genuinely impressed, touching his thinning hair like a man checking to see if his hat had blown off in the wind.

He didn't talk back to his dad the way I did to mine, not even under his breath. "He's got it hard," he told me, "can't really breathe."

"He needs to lose some weight," I diagnosed.

"We all need to lose something."

"Careful. You're starting to sound like a country song."

"I like country."

O.'s father shot himself in the head three weeks before my brother died. He did it in the backyard, leaning against the house. "Ruined the paint," O. told me a few days later. He had the stunned expression of a mummy, his skin tight against his head. And it wasn't from being high. "Mom came home. She wasn't happy." Things must be removed, I thought. For beauty to be revealed. But what if there is no beauty? What if there is only revelation without understanding? Or clarity with only ugliness? It took the war to tell me that it wasn't beauty that was being revealed.

O.'s mom left a week later. She took the girls and their braces and mean jokes. She let O. remain in the house to finish his senior year. But at my brother's funeral, before the service even started, he pulled me aside. The corners of his mouth fishhooked down to bite off the tears. "I can't stay here," he said. He put his hand on the top of my head, almost said something, then turned and left the church. I never saw him again. The FOR SALE sign went up. The shades came down.

And no one heard from O. Like he'd never existed. He had never been to my house. I didn't like people breathing the toxins of my father's spent cigarettes and relentless silence. O. was an outsider at school, like me. Anyone at his house who knew me was gone to somewhere else. I wondered for months how I could even prove there was an O. It became too important, occupying my thoughts like scores in a gambler's head.

The paint, I finally remembered. I dug through the garage and found my scraper, still yellowed from the job. For a moment I thought about driving Mom over, explaining who O. was, what we'd done to the house, creating proof of the friendship by speaking it out loud. But I knew she'd end up saying, "You miss your brother, that's all." But that was not all. O. had been a friend. And even if he didn't want to say good-bye, keep in touch, be remembered to me, I needed to know I was capable of kindness. Trust. That someone outside my family, someone who didn't have to care about me, actually did. At least for a time.

I parked across the street. Same address. Same lemon tree in the yard. But this house was white. Perfect, pearled white. The name on the mailbox had changed, the sale sign plucked and replanted somewhere else. I held my scraper before my eyes, then looked at the thick whiteness in front of me. There was no one home. I ran around behind the house and started scraping.

They'd layered on gallons, and the work was difficult. My shoulders and back strained, sweat across my forehead lining up like abacus beads. I was still scraping when I heard a car pull into the drive. Faster. Deeper. Finally. Underneath the whitewash bled a fine vein of our peacock plum. At this level, the white finally opened, and the color bloomed out like a slow wound. I could also see the stain that O.'s father had left behind. I chose this spot not to hide but to reveal. That a life was lived in this house. A life ended. And a friend came and went. Departure would not be forgetting. It would be remembering.

And Mom would have been right. I did miss my little brother. I leaned against the house, the paint stripped away so the memories could breathe, and I wept for my brother. And O.'s dad. And even for O. For what was gone. Because gone was all I had.

A violent pothole in the road jerked me out of memory and up to the top of the windshield. I exhaled a small grunt from the impact. "Didn't think you were asleep." The driver's voice was as familiar and sickening as a vaccination. Mc. I still refused to acknowledge him. I hated that I had failed to kill him. That he was leashing me around. To the hotel, as if to save me, now on the road to some other version of oblivion. It was starting to irritate me that he was keeping me alive.

"You act like we've never been friends," he said. His voice had the deep tenor of teasing that my father had used to humiliate me and my brother. Cruel familiarity. Yeah, I'm an asshole, it seemed to say. What're you gonna do about it? Nothing. You're gonna do nothing.

I stared out the window again. "Ever play car games when you were a kid? And don't give me that bullshit, sad-sack-of-shit-soldier answer, 'I was never a kid.' Everybody was a kid. Even God." I could tell he was looking at me while he was talking. I was hoping he'd not notice something in the road and plow into it. But there was nothing. The emptiness out the passenger window and windshield was almost lunar in its perfection.

I had seen the photos in newspapers, of every far-flung war, civil or uncivil, since I was a kid. Always someone anonymously bleeding, the women wailing, their mouths smeared with grief. Often there was a dust-covered man hurrying away from the photographer, as if late for an appointment. And every one I'd ever seen had seemed utterly staged to me. The light, the squared horror, the containment of so much anguish in such a tiny space, seemed as artificial as cotton candy. Why the fuck would anyone with a camera want to get that close to such a thing? He should have been helping or fleeing, not goddamn clicking away. So instead of trying to find logic in the situation, I found artifice. Pictures lied. The only way to see something that brutal was to stand in the middle of it and remember.

But as I looked out at the rubbled silence of this war, I finally understood the reason for those photographs. Someone had to capture the moment between hope and decimation because, by the time something like this ended, no one who'd seen anything worth remembering would be left to tell the story. Yes, photographers were thieves. But they were stealing from history so there would be proof that life had even passed through a certain place and time.

"What did they want from us?" I finally asked. The question came clear and bold. It made me sit up, though I still didn't square to Mc. "What was our purpose? To just fucking drink, wait to die?"

"*Is*, soldier," he answered. "What *is* our purpose. This ain't some past tense we're driving through. I'm sorry you saw what you saw, but you are more in this than the day they recruited your angry ass. So don't pretend you're not here. Or you're lost, or anyone's victim. Be alive, soldier, while you can. Everything after is just going to . . ." He didn't finish, and it made me look at him. The muscles in his jaw pulsed beneath his skin. He didn't want to die. Maybe I did have something over him after all. But I'd have to get close enough this time to get a bullet closer to his heart. And for that I'd need his gun, so I'd humor him.

"I miss the old Mc.," I said. "The one with the bad jokes and endless stories."

"They weren't all bad."

"They were. *Bad* is generous." I felt a smile conspire against my lips, and I couldn't tell if it was part of my act, or if Mc. was really that magnetic.

"I've got plenty, if you're looking to pass the time."

"Is there a lot? Of time?" I gazed out the windshield again.

"Probably not."

"Are we driving toward or away?" I asked. "Not that it matters."

He answered with a joke. It was a new one or, if not new, then one he hadn't wasted on me before. It was filled with elaborate pauses, his trademark repetitions, and a squandered punch line involving a cow. When he finished he turned to me with the need for approval my brother used to show after doing a somersault, aged five. It was this kind of humanity in Mc. that kept fucking me up.

"It isn't funny."

"Then why are you grinning?"

"Disbelief." The joke bought us ten minutes of silence.

"Never had a friend till the army."

"Are we in the army?" I asked.

"Military. Whatever. Never had any idea I was funny."

"Repeat. You are not."

"People listen, then they laugh. That's the definition."

"It could be derision."

"It's not." He was right. He knew he had that thing that made people pay attention. Give him their trust. It was how he'd been able to fool us all.

"You blew up the hotel, Mc. I know. I saw everybody dead."

"You saw what you saw. Can't seem to talk you out of that." He let the steering wheel slide between his fingers like a gardener letting out hose. The car gripped and spit over a sudden chop in the road, and then he held the wheel firm again. "People see all manner of things in situations like this. Their past, their future. Hell, I thought I saw Mother Mary herself standing over me like a warning. Or a wish." He stopped, shook his head like an old man who'd seen too much suffering to do anything but be amazed.

"You believe in that? All that?"

"Hell, I'm Irish Catholic, boyo. It's not a belief. It's a tattoo."

"I'm afraid," I said, against my will. And a surge of tears was stopped only by the dam of my will.

"Me, too," Mc. said, but flat. Like the weather report. I didn't believe him. I started to reach to strangle him, to crash us, to do something besides this friendly banter, this compassionate empathetic bullshit drive. "Don't," he said, intercepting my intent like a cartoon character putting his finger into a pistol. It worked. Mc. had a force field around him, and I had still not located the Achilles door. "There." He pointed and swerved at the same moment, tiring up dust at the harshness of the turn. "See it?" He sped up, then slowed down, his eyes on the dashboard. "This is good. This is important."

"Why?" I asked.

"Because we're out of gas."

Mc. raced to a stop alongside a row of gasoline pumps. The pole that held the sign had melted into a shepherd's staff of metal, and all the identifiable markers on the pumps themselves had been burned away by a localized, supreme heat.

"Why didn't this place blow?" I asked as I stepped out of the vehicle. It was the first time I noticed we were in a peacekeeper field vehicle. The logo on my door had not yet been erased by the war.

"Gasoline's underground," Mc. explained. "Either that, or there ain't none left."

The pumps were all that was standing. The cashier booth was a bump of remains twenty-five feet away.

"Where'd you get the truck?" I said, lifting the pump as if I worked there. I jiggered it up and down, but it yielded only the faintest click. The nozzle had been pinched smaller by the attack, but it was still wide enough to sneak gas through. If there had been gas. "Empty," I said, jamming the arm back into its metal sleeve.

"Not empty," said Mc., squinting into the dirt-smeared Plexiglas face of the pump. "Probably pay before pumping. How hilarious is that?" Mc. checked the other two pumps, the futile clicking their only response. "It's under here. I know it."

Mc. got on all fours to examine the base of the pumps. They had been sealed to the ground, but bombs had crumbled the concrete like stale cookies, and he was looking for an entry. I could have charged him and kicked his ribs through his shirt, but I had come to believe he was either invincible or necessary. The prospect of being out there alone again, without any more answers, kept my violence in check.

"Again. Where'd you get a peacekeeper truck?"

"See if there's a crowbar in the back," he said, eyes peering into a cynosure of ground. "I think we can jimmy this up. And I can smell the fumes. It's down here."

Crowbar. If I found one, then I wouldn't need the surprise attack. I could stand over him like a surgical nurse and hand it to the back of his head. Instead, I found the crowbar and gave it to him. He never even glanced up, his shoulders never tensed. He knew I needed him. That was his armor. And that's why he was keeping me ignorant, avoiding my questions, treating me like a neighborhood child.

"Now," he said, rising, the crowbar jammed in at a thirty-degree angle beneath the pump. "Let's pry this open."

The gasoline came out as if from a water gun. It hit Mc. square in the chest, inking his shirt with a circle that extended to his belt. And we both fell back laughing. There was no way to stop the fountain. We couldn't get our hands in close enough without enjoying a petroleum mouth rinse. Mc. reparked the truck and chose our only remaining option. I opened the gas tank, he lined it up, and we let the truck drink from the fountain. We watched and laughed, the laughter as odd as applause in a cemetery. Mc. slapped my back. I punched his arm. We were stupid and giddy, and soon the tank was full, the excess dribbling down from the gas tank like booze from a drunk's chin.

And still the fountain. We'd hit a vein deep enough to fill a parking lot of trucks. "We should be harvesting this," I said. "And selling it."

"With what, to who?" Mc. countered, his snort sneaking through the traffic of his teeth. "My fucking shirt." Mc. took it off and knotted it to the roof rack to dry on the drive. He pulled out an extra from a rucksack in the backseat.

"Anything else in there? Like food?"

"No food. Besides, everyone knows this war's about oil," he mocked.

"Is that this war?"

"Does it matter?"

"Maybe," I said. "Because this could mean we won." We managed a few final chuckles. The spout finally pissed itself dry and there came the feeling of night. Mc. threw me the keys.

"You drive. I'm tired." We got in, started up. "Don't kill me in my sleep or you'll never get where you're going."

"Where am I going?"

"Just drive, and —"

"I know. I know . . . kill you in your sleep."

"That's *don't* kill, kid," he challenged, already tucking himself in to rest. "Careful. Leave out a word, the wrong word . . ."

Don't kill, I said to myself. Come to a war and don't kill the one guy you want to kill. Just drive. And maybe, maybe stay alive.

Being lost is a type of liberation. Destinations create impatience, worry, expectations, disappointments. With Mc. asleep beside me and the night storing away the day, I felt I could drive myself past the edges and the imaginings. In the subtle darkness, I could see the humming outlines of everything that had been burned away. The ghosts of buildings and schoolhouses. The ashes of arenas, the pummeled parking lots, the invisible skyscrapers. This place had become placeless. Stripped of all identifiers, it was now a pure thing. Gone were the magazines and the newspapers. Fliers stuck to telephone poles seeking the missing were now missing themselves. I was driving across a landscape so ruined that it was new. Pre. Uncluttered. And man's genius at destruction begged for nothing ever to be rebuilt here again.

War had edited it down to the essentials. Air, earth, sea, fire. War had simplified the extraneous wastefulness of man. It had taken the flavor of personality and flattened it, spread it so thin it removed even a taste, a hint. I was nowhere.

And then I remembered music. Like most memories, it was stoked by the lack of the thing. Absence doesn't make anything grow fonder, it makes things more present. For we never notice a thing more intently than when we want it and it is denied. Mc. had stirred, and his mouth leaked a few hummed notes from inside the chamber of his slumber. That made me reach for the radio. It had been sitting there in the dash the whole time, but it hadn't occurred to me that there might be some information out there I could steal while my friendly captor slept. Click. I kept the volume infinitesimal, so that the static and popcorn crackle wouldn't rouse Mc. I spun the dial like a roulette wheel. Only need one. Just one station. Come on, come on. Turn, turn . . .

The composer was German. From Leipzig. Or Berlin? I recalled not knowing the answer when it was on a high-school test. It didn't matter where he was from, did it? I had complained at the time. Home is just a place one is sentenced to. Or, for happier people, a place one gets loaned, a gift with an expiration date. But my music teacher had found it fundamental, this composer's place of birth. Gave me a thousand throaty recitations of the village, hamlet, city, burg. And I still forgot. Out of spite, I am certain. My teacher had a way of making you hate everything she liked. She wore her hair so tight it was a punishment. Her glasses fogged when she was mad at a student, as if her eyes exhaled toxic gases. I despised everything about the class except for this one composer. The fromless German. This man who had been born so many hundreds of years before me that he could easily have been a lie. Except his music (and it was his, it belonged to no one else, no one armed with notes and pencil and imagination had ever come close) told the truth. No. *Was* the truth. Or seemed to be the truth as long as I was listening to it. Ultimately, I had plugged my ears to him, because when the music finished I was lost. I needed his truth to be not just guide but map as well.

And it never passed over into my silence. This oxygen he gave always sealed shut when the record stopped. So I thought, if that is what you do with truth, if it is only a seduction, an invitation, and the rest you have to figure out yourself, then fuck it. Rather not know at all. Better to stay blind, stay blind than to see for a moment and then have the darkness return. For years I hated this man who began to tell me he knew what it felt like to be me but never finished the explanation.

I hadn't heard one phrase of his compositions since the night I'd played it for my ex-wife. We were near the end, though she didn't know it. And I'd played the record as a bridge for her to walk across. If she heard what I heard, if she could understand even half of the safety and promise I experienced, then maybe she could teach me to live in the gaps between the notes.

But she talked while I needed her to listen. She made

tea, she stroked my face. She loved me. But she didn't listen, didn't obey the rules of my secret, nasty game. So I killed the music. And soon escaped her love. I had always been expert at eliminating beauty. It's why I felt custom-built for war. But now, in the face of all that nothing, I suddenly longed for beauty. Even a droplet. It didn't matter how long it lasted. I nudged the volume with my index finger. Notch by notch, keeping watch over the sleeping Mc., until I could hear all the orchestrated splendor slipping up above the rattle of car and road. Surfacing like a reverse angel, the music shimmering on the brightest wings.

I can't describe the rest. Or won't. But for the moments that followed (as many as there were until Mc. snapped awake like a man chased in his dreams and I snapped off the radio to hoard my epiphany) I was OK. I was almost . . . I thought I might be . . . OK.

"Why are you crying?" Mc. asked, curiously, not mockingly.

"Bonn. It's a town in Germany." I finally remembered.

"Yeah?"

"There's a small street in the city center. Close to everything. That's where a friend of mine was born."

I stared at the black canvas of night that we were painting our way across with high beams of halogen and hope. I kept thinking we were going to hit something, arrive on an edge, tumble off like a fatigued lemming eager for the splash. "I feel like Columbus," I said. "I'm suddenly terrified that the world is flat."

"It's not," Mc. countered.

"First time, Mc." I had to yield. "Actually funny." Mc. popped open the glove compartment and procured a pack of cigarettes and a lighter. I didn't smoke, but it still seemed as if he'd discovered a hidden treasure. He lit one and passed it to me. All soldiers smoke when offered. It's the eleventh commandment. "Did you know?" I asked.

"Should've guessed. This is a Euro truck."

"Tastes amazing." I coughed but meant it. The tobacco was the first food I'd had in I couldn't keep track of how long. My stomach grumbled, and I took a deeper drag. "Where did you . . ."

"Get the truck. Right. Never answered that," Mc. admitted. The embered cigarette gave him a tiny campfire glow. Made his hard-scraped features softer.

"Never answered anything."

"Yeah," he exhaled. "Guess not." We smoked in silence. Was it a dare? Another bad joke? Finally, "He wanted to kill you, so I killed him. Took the truck. Left. Staying didn't seem the wise choice. Although leaving's not looking too good at the moment either." At last I realized that Mc. reminded me of politicians back home. They answered questions that hadn't been asked with words that begged other questions they wouldn't answer. They made themselves geniuses by making everyone else feel stupid. But this time I was going to probe. "Who?"

"Who what?"

"Mc., I will crash this fucking vehicle."

"Good. Break up the monotony."

I jerked hard enough to lift us off one wheel, but I needed something to smash into if I was going to flip the truck.

"OK, but this isn't because you're a shitty driver," he explained, putting his smoke out on the dash and blistering the plastic. "This is just . . . because . . . I'm going to tell you this."

Life is so different when you expect to be lied to. Otherwise, when Mc. started with "I can only tell you what I know," I would have slowed down and eagerly soaked up every morbid detail. Instead I sped up with each sentence, pretending the lies were pressing the accelerator and when he reached the apex we would burst into flames. And he never mentioned our hurtling speed, just kept spilling broken sentences like an animal spitting out bones. "It all comes back to what everyone's assignment is. Was. Is. You get it. I had mine. You had yours. I mean, R. must have said something to you when he shoved you out the door."

I didn't answer. He wanted to be private, I didn't need to tell him that the exact wording of my mission was "Go." Maybe it was clearer to everyone else. But I hadn't known what the fuck I was doing since the day I'd arrived, blind-folded and thirsty. I was on an escalator, couldn't even say up or down, and if obedience would give order to my life, then I was willing to stay on my step, inside their parameters. But obedience had only led to more chaos. And while Mc. raved his lies like a street-corner preacher without faith, all my questions began to shave down to one: Why am I still alive?

If there was no rhythm or crescendo to this battle we were in the middle of, then maybe I just needed to figure out the personal so I could slip through the gap. That had to be the way out. Know why, then die. I had no illusions about discovering my place and being sent back home a hero. I didn't picture myself standing on a pile of enemy bones, waiting for war photographers to drift by and flash me across the global transom. And a man without goals is just waiting to die anyway. What I did learn from Mc. was that I didn't need him. He didn't have a scintilla of my facts, any facts, and, if he did, not even torture would get him to share them.

"Absolutely," I murmured. "Fascinating."

"You still don't believe me because you think I torched the hotel."

"Mc., I don't believe you because I don't believe you."

He liked that one, couldn't hide it. He took a glance at the speedometer. "Fast won't scare me."

"Not trying to scare you, Red. Trying to scare myself." I pinned it past eighty, and the truck entered a synchronicity of bumpiness that almost felt smooth. For a second I had the sensation we were sliding on ice into the gaping mouth of an invisible forest. I became certain we would hit a fir tree or a startled buck any instant. "I used to drive at night with the lights out," I confessed. "Three a.m., sneak out, and drive crazy down my street. Hoping to hit something. See what it felt like."

"Feels like shit, I imagine," Mc. said. His voice had its first quiver, and he locked his fingers around whatever surface would allow it.

"There are things I've done no one will ever know."

"True for all of us, bleeder."

"Why do you keep calling me bleeder? We're the same age. You're younger, even. Same goddamn rank."

"No," he said.

"You think I bought that shit about you being my CO? When you open your mouth, you lie," I berated. Then, slowly, as if to a child or a government worker, "Do you understand my lack of faith?"

"I helped recruit you, ————," and he said my name. My full name. First, middle, last. He named the woman in the diner. The tight collar at the bar. The beard of bees at the grocery store. "I was on the committee that chose you, son. So I think I'm qualified to say whether you are still bleeding or not."

My foot came off the gas. I didn't brake, just let the car find its slowness. Lies, I reminded myself. They're only more lies. I had told Mc. about my recruitment in a drunken haze during early days in the hotel. Or I had told another who told Mc. Maybe I sleepwalked, sleeptalked, and shouted it from the lobby up the stairs until all of us knew exactly the road I'd taken.

Bullshit. I knew I'd never spoken to anyone about the details. We weren't men with pasts worth remembering, certainly not worth swapping as anecdotes. I took the job to be concealed, not revealed. I just hadn't stopped to think that somebody besides R. knew the details. That there was a higher-up in our lowly midst. Mc. had been a spy. But not for the enemy. He'd been inside the hotel to make sure everything went smoothly, and he'd returned feigning injury to see how we all handled that.

"Are you my CO?"

"Yes." And suddenly he didn't look like a boy full of mischief and mayhem. He looked like a leader. He looked like he knew the way.

"Why did you blow up the hotel?"

"I did not. Enemy bomb."

"Why did we leave? The second hotel. Why did you punch me?"

"It wasn't safe anymore. You shouldn't have seen that map."

"What was it a map of?"

"My job is to protect my men," he recited. "I will take a thousand bullets to protect my men."

"But everybody's dead."

"Not everybody." The truck stopped. The engine idled quietly, ready to roar, happy to be catching its breath. Mc. pulled me another smoke without my needing to ask. This one tasted like a mistake, but I smoked it anyway. Down till it burned the quick of my nails.

"I want to do something," I said. "Aim a gun. Drop a bomb. Something."

"Soldiering is mostly reaction. Rarely action."

"What if I'm not a soldier?"

"You are."

"Not a good soldier."

"All soldiers are good soldiers."

"Feel like I cannot be . . . the best soldier without more information."

"You went out. You got lost. You got found. Now you're with me. That's all you need to know."

"Where is everyone? Where is the enemy? Which way do we go?"

"Forward, son. Always forward." I turned off the engine. "Not a good idea," he said.

"I want to wait here. Wait for daylight. I need to see where we are."

"In the combat zone, probably with a target on our back. Move out." I popped the keys out of the ignition and stepped into the dark. The headlamps' tubes of light were the only visible shape. Even the truck seemed to vanish back away from the hood. Mc. remained in the passenger seat. "Soldier," he said, "enough."

"Exactly." I concurred, then threw the keys as deep into the darkness as my stiffened shoulder would allow. With Mc. bolting out and slamming the door, I couldn't even hear where they landed. "Guess we're staying here. Till daylight, sir." Mc.'s face looked hollowed out in the half-light. As if someone had taken a scoop from his cheekbone to his chin. He started to speak, guttural and raw, words instead of punches, but I cut him off with a confidence I hadn't felt all day. "Don't worry about dying out here. That's the thing I seem to do worst of all."

"Soldier, you are disobeying a direct order," he barked.

"I hope so."

"If you endanger your fellow soldier."

"You're not my fellow. My compatriot. My anything. Fuck off, then," I said. "Fuck off with your placeless maps and your need-to-know." He seemed to lose power as I surged with it. "I don't need you to rescue me, kidnap me, whatever the fuck . . ."

Mc. lowered his chin and his voice, as if he didn't want to hear himself speak. "I have an obligation."

"You are relieved of it," I said.

"I got you this far."

"I don't want to go any farther," I admitted. Exhaustion like an injury.

"You'll have to." Face still downcast. "We will both have to —"

"What, soldier on?" I mocked. "Not me, Mc. Soldier your own goddamn self on." I didn't wait to see if my words had done their intended work. I climbed into the back of the truck, and before Mc. even moved I was fast asleep. And dreamless.

Amnesia. Not permanent, barely even real, but sleep was always dusted with the edges of amnesia, so that waking up was a borning. And for the seconds before I realized where or when I was, I was back in the cradle. New. Possibility personified. Breathing free.

When I finally awoke, my hand was so close to my eyes that my fingertips appeared to me a baby's hand. My own infant hand. The lines of the prints were recently etched by God's tender knife, and the skin was pink as the inside of an orchid. I opened and closed my eyes, letting the lashes fall like palm branches in an easy breeze. Not that I had been born on an island or even had any memories before falling out of a tree when I was six, but that was the sweet lie of such an awakening amnesia. Not only did I forget what I would be waking to, I forgot everything that had come before.

Sun slanted in through the window, making thin pillars of light between my baby fingers. The open palm of my hand had barely visible lines. No signs of worry or wear. And the flesh was plump and round with newness. I drew my thumb in, examining the joint with the wonder of discovery, then balled it all into a gentle fist and tried to fall back asleep. But the odor wouldn't let me.

Gasoline. That was not the aroma of a newborn's crib. It was the dried stench of Mc.'s shirt in the backseat. Mc. must've taken it off the roof rack and slid it under my head as a pillow. But now it had fallen into the crook of my neck, where the vapors rose up like smelling salts. Amnesia gone, war on.

I jerked up in one motion, a man late for work, and saw that I was alone. The day was brighter than I'd seen since leaving the hotel, but small dark clouds moved like stones across the lake of sky. "Mc.," I said instinctively. The door cracked open and I tested my injured leg on the ground. The wound was tight as drum skin, but the pain was muted and I walk-limped to the front of the vehicle. "Mc." A little louder as I three-sixtied the view. Nothing. In the far distance, what had to be an electrical tower standing at the end of things like a giant, lost giraffe. For a moment I guessed Mc. had to be out looking for the keys, but it wasn't possible that I'd thrown them so far that finding them would lead to a disappearance. Had he abandoned me? Grown tired of my complaints and distrust? I viewed the landscape again, more rapidly, my heart beginning to trip like the heart of a child forgotten at a rest stop. It was a feeling I knew better than a simile.

I walked toward where I could best recall throwing the keys. In the daylight, the ground was easier to navigate without rolling an ankle. The road, or what was left of it, was devoured and pale. Even the macadam had had the color scared out of it by all the attacks. With each step I cast a glance back to the truck. Ever since R. had found me in the sea, I had been with someone, off and on, for the bulk of the last days. Being suddenly alone, without walls or weapon, without means of escape, felt like being naked from the inside out. Even my thoughts seemed exposed. They know I'm afraid, I imagined. Whoever's out there, they are laughing. Waiting. And they already have the keys.

But they didn't. I stepped right on them, and then I was the one laughing. And running back to the truck, get in, lock the doors, start the engine. I was explaining the actions to my body, just in case.

The engine turned over, and I put it into gear. Sideways, I thought. That's the gear I wanted. That way I could sneak out of there without anyone noticing. First, clutch. Reverse. Clutch. First. Reverse. My right foot poised over the gas. But, unwilling to flex, I turned off the engine. Then the flat sun caught the top of the electrical tower like the wink of a beautiful woman, and I had my destination. As for Mc., wherever the hell he was, he'd have to walk.

I drove so fast, the light coming in through the side windows became nauseating. The truck's shocks were shot, so the undercarriage scraped and sparked and my head met the thin metal roof often enough to leave more than a small impression.

The tower came closer and closer, and, on the tiny smooth patches of road, it seemed it was hurrying to me. The power lines that had formerly stretched for electric miles now hung like thin hair from the tower's once-proud head. A hundred feet tall and useless, the tower offered no sanctuary. No strategic benefit, no nourishment or hideaway. It was simply a visible destination. And I hoped that, like the Sphinx, its mere presence would offer something new. Even if it was only more questions. I was beginning to feel protective of my questions. They were the only things that hadn't abandoned me.

My speed and my distraction added up to my sudden arrival. Even slamming on the brakes couldn't keep me from sideswiping the base of the tower and taking a deep dent in the passenger-side door. I left the engine running and got out. From directly below, the tower seemed more alive. Long metal beams like arms crossed and angry. Wide feet slanted in the earth, jointless legs rising to a torso of unbending steel. I had questions, but this tower had desires as well. It wanted to be climbed. And I needed the view.

The footholds and hand grips had all been prefabbed into the apparatus, so ascending was easier than if I had been on a playground. I monkey-climbed it so fast, my feet didn't have time to slip, nor my legs ache for a moment. The higher I climbed, the surer I was that this was my Sphinx and climbing was the answer to the riddle. I would get to the top and finally see what was out there. See far enough to identify or, at the very least, far enough to know which direction was next.

Ever since falling from that tree at six (the distance of which had increased in my memory every year since), I had been terrified of climbing. Wouldn't even climb the ladder to take the slide down like other kids. I'd run up its tongue to reach the top. But these days had taught me that necessity erases fear. At least long enough to execute the action. And as I clambered up and up, the vast nothing below me, the pinnacle and its promise above me, I was weightless. Fearless. With enough steps, I could have climbed up to the sun to see how close a man could get and live.

Only twenty feet to go, and I felt so connected to the metal that it seemed I *was* metal. I didn't need to hold onto any surface, I had become a part of it. Will was adhering me and gravity could not pull me off. A gust blew through the skeleton, setting off an archaic whistling, an ancient modern song. I hummed the tune to myself all the way to the apex. But I didn't stop. I climbed up past the top until I was clutching air like a cartoon villain. Needed my feet and knees to pinch in or my climb would have been remembered by no one but the wind. And as I caught myself, I caught my breath. And with it, wrangled my fear. "Don't look down," I puffed, lungs burning like a prophet's lips. I closed my eyes, but that just made the sway deeper. The tower now felt like a single needle stuck into the earth, and I the idiot angel, trying not to dance off its edge.

My fingers dug in to the metal until blood pressed out over certain edges. Metal no more. Human. Frightened human. How the fuck was I going to get down? But before that, calm yourself. Get some use out of this suicide ascension. Open your eyes. Look. If you're so goddamn eager to see, you're going to have to look.

A thousand soldiers. But only that number because it was at least that, and more didn't matter. What could matter more than a thousand against one? Not that they were against me. I was pretty certain they couldn't see me, and if they did from their distance, they wouldn't have trusted that what they saw clinging to the top of the tower like the harvest's final apple was a man at all.

And soldiers never look up. We were taught to look for kill shots on the enemy and at our own feet so as not to fall and bring down all those rushing behind in formation. Or to guess at land mines and dance in between. No good soldier ever looked up. If a bomb was dropping, it was already too late. Survival was at eye level. Anything else was the margin. And life was not maintained on the margins.

The soldiers were scattered enough for me to see that they were not one battalion but a few joined together for this attack. Their uniforms were indistinguishable from such a height. They appeared as insects, rushing, hoping to avoid the heel of time. I judged that if I descended as rapidly as I had risen, I could get to the truck in time to escape. But one look down and the accompanying wave of nausea said that was an improbable outcome.

"Get down here," my father said. "Ass down here or I will push you out of this goddamn tree." I looked at the soldiers, their approach erratic yet true. Then I looked down again. My father wasn't there. But the wind had found his voice and carried it up to me. "Oh, I get it." His voice as raspy as a train announcement. "Kid's afraid. Hey, honey, your son knows how to climb up, but he's too scared to come down. Maybe he's a daughter."

The smooth metal of the tower turned to knobbed branches. A flag of leaves clothed my face and I hid behind it. "He's deaf, your daughter," he yelled toward the house, where my mother stood helpless in the doorway. She was kneading a tea towel like a set of rosary beads. And then he started to climb. I could hear the grunts of anger, the gum stick of his shoe sole on the withered bark. He wasn't very good, but he was strong enough to climb, and he was coming up to throw me out.

I restraddled the tower, which had become slicker as wood, and I could feel fatigue fevering into my muscles. "Here I come, you little pain in the ass. Looks like it might be a long drop. Gonna hurt," he snorted, the tar in his lungs squeezing his breath out in short geysers. "That'll be the first punishment."

"I'm not coming," I protested, my voice fragile as a glass in a drunkard's hand. "Leave me alone." I couldn't tell him the reason I was late for dinner stuck up in this tree was because I was too afraid to climb down. He'd never have forgiven, nor stopped reminding me. It needed to be diso-bedience. That would engender a beating that would stop hurting in a day or two. Admitting fear meant fifteen straight years of humiliation and pain.

"Leave him, then," my mother said, feigning anger with me. "Let him eat acorns for dinner." But it didn't stop my father. He was only a limb below me, and I could see his splotched face, red as a tourist's.

Jump, I had thought. Just jump. That'll scare the shit out of him. "Hey," I said quietly enough so only he could hear.

"Watch this." And I let go. I fell too speedily to see his face on the way down, but I liked to imagine it over the years. I bet it was the one time he actually looked worried about me. Sorry. Caught. But soon I was the one caught. By hard earth and the oak's knuckled roots.

My mother had reached me first, my father having just as much trouble getting down as I had imagined I would. His shirt snagged and tore on a stiff branch and I laughed as long as my broken ribs would let me. "That hurt," I said.

"What did I do?" Mom said to me. She wanted to run in and call an ambulance but didn't want to leave me alone for my father's arrival. He landed with a toppled inefficiency before I could answer. When he stood over me, he appeared to want to kick me back into the house. "Go call," Mom said to him. "This is your fault." My father didn't look at her. He kept his shame buried and then glared it into me before sidling back to the house. Slowly.

Mom knelt beside me, stroked my hair as apology. "You shouldn't, you know," she said. Meaning climb, challenge your father, embarrass him that way.

"I'll try," I whispered through the pain of what would turn out to be three broken ribs and a separated shoulder, a lucky result.

"You coming down or not, candy-ass?" he said again, up in the high-wind cool of the morning. I could see the thousand soldiers closing. See that their uniforms were not the same as mine. "Hey, Dad. Watch this."

In my mind, I let go. But I was tired of almost dying and not ready to let my last mistake be caused by the memory of an asshole. So I climbed. Down. Not expertly. Not with legendary speed. Yet I somehow managed a foothold at a time, keeping an eye on the hurrying horizon of guns and ammo. Down, down, like a boy from a bunk bed in a stranger's house. Searching for the next step with the tips of my toes. Finding a rhythm, faster, faster as I went.

By the time I touched soil, the soldiers were close enough to start firing. Getting in the vehicle, glass sparkled across my lap like diamonds after a robbery. I circle-reversed as their bullets pinged and skewered their way into the metal, but not into me. Not the tires, I thought, or prayed, or wished. All three were answered. I raced away from the tower, shifting gears in smooth succession, checking the rearview to ensure the final bullet wasn't gaining on me. Letting all the faster violence pass on the left.

The climb hadn't given me what I had hoped: a direction to go in. But it had given me one to flee. So I drove. Full tank of gas. No traffic. Even found the one radio station again. But it wasn't playing music. There was a man speaking and then a woman. A flurry of conversation. In a language I did not understand.

I drove, I listened. Tried to ascertain the language by cadence or emphasis. But long pauses were countered by rapid
exchanges, then laughter, then tidbits of a third voice. Despite the arguing, they all, somehow, seemed to be agreeing.
After another hearty conspiratorial laugh from the woman,
I turned them all off and buckled my seat belt.

If it had been meant to disorient, it had worked. Because
even in the switching off, with my eyes glancing down to eye
the knob, I had failed to see the horse. Or that it was lying in
what I had thought was the street. Or that it had already
been torn in half.

I collared the steering wheel hard left to avoid the head,
catching just enough of the horse's prone shoulder to put
me up on three wheels. From there, with the wheel cranked
so hard, it was a short distance to two wheels, even shorter
to none. At fifty miles an hour, I scraped, driver's side
down, along the hard-scrabble terrain. I shed the window,
then my uniform along the shoulder and back, then the
skin, rubbed off like the silver on a losing lottery ticket. I
screamed, but the metal screamed louder, until we both
stopped.

"Never took a seat belt off a dead man" was a line I'd
heard on a television show as a kid. A paramedic was explaining it to a group of children who'd been scared straight
by a gruesome video montage of car crashes. I'd found the
man who said this both disingenuous and cruel. He seemed

to relish the term "dead man" and enjoy how terrified the little children appeared. But, like him or not, I'd always obeyed the slick-haired, mustached EMT. And on that particular day, I thanked him for my life.

I unclicked the belt and hoisted my relatively uninjured (save for the filet of shoulder and shoulder blade) body out through the passenger-side window. I examined all my limbs like a factory worker testing a robot on the assembly line. All bent, all worked. The air was bright on my peeled shoulder, but the rest of me felt blessed. Then pissed. What the hell was a horse, no, half a horse, doing in the middle of the street? I walked back toward the dead animal, as if it were a fellow driver who'd cut me off on the thoroughfare, and information and profanities needed to be exchanged.

The horse had no defense to offer. Its snout had flattened so that the nostrils were both on the same plane. Its innards had long ago dried under the ceaseless sky. Not even the flies could be bothered anymore. The gap where the rest of the horse should have been was as shocking as the horse's presence itself. It almost looked as if it had been sawn in half. Though by whom, and with what instrument, was just another minor question sliding onto my list. I got as close as the stink would allow, but the only fact that became clearer was that this had been an old horse. A workhorse. The kind of horse rented to kids and first-time riders. The cut of its mane, the weathered sheen of its shoulders and back said this animal had lived a long life and carried its share of the load. A workhorse, in the middle of a city. A tourist's horse, torn asunder in the midst of a chaotic, urban war. Was I in a city where horse was on the menu? Possible. But this one hadn't been meat to anyone. This was a packhorse. An old Belgian draft. A doer. And with its expression pinned to the ground, it looked just as surprised as I.

Then I heard them. The thousand soldiers. I'd driven maybe two miles before the overturn, and that meant they were advancing at a sprint. I could hear the collective kick of their running, the low baritone of their war song, the straightforward march of their vengeance.

I tried, uselessly, to right the truck. Come on, be heroic, I prodded myself, but the truck was asleep, and there would be no rousing it. I couldn't yet see the enemy, so I thought if I could move away from them on foot at the same speed, my head start would still be enough. And so I bent over and touched my toes like a high-school cross-country runner, inhaled oxygen for vitamins, and tore ass out of there.

Running, despite the pricks of pain in leg and back, did make me feel like a kid again. Chasing my little brother through the backyard leaves, making sure to screw up all the neat piles we'd organized under Father's supervision.

Running for gym class in high school, where I would pick out the kid that was on the track team and outrun him in speed and distance just to make him feel as shitty as I did twenty-three hours of the day. More than once, the track coach asked me why I wouldn't try out for the team. "I just did," I said.

"Damn right," he agreed. "And you made it." He had an Adam's apple that bounced up and down like a carnival game.

"Coach, the only time I run is when something's chasing me."

"But you just ran right now. Outran my best guy."

"Just because you didn't see it," I smiled, happy to be confusing him, "doesn't mean it wasn't there." That comment and attendant slyness got me a mandatory sit-down with the school's mental-health counselor, a woman of such resolute stiffness she appeared to have been bathed at the dry cleaner. At the end of it she concluded there was nothing wrong with me.

"You're really good at your job," I told her. "What are you doing at a little high school like this?"

"I ask myself that question all the time," she said, the thin smile nearly cracking her face.

"Keep asking," I told her. "Repetition always helps me calm down when I don't know what the hell's going on." I rose, offered my hand, and let her walk me to the door, our hands still linked.

"I wish there was something wrong with you, Mr. ———. That way I'd get to talk to you a lot more."

"What're you gonna do, doc? Being healthy's a bitch. Nothing to complain about. No one to listen. I'll tell you, it's no goddamn picnic." My cursing crowbarred her smile open a tiny bit wider. She scolded me with her eyes, then returned me into the hall, her hand like an oven mitt easing me back into the oven.

The next week I saw track coach in the hallway. He greeted me like an uncle on holiday. "Hear you got everything straightened out with the psych. Ready to run?" He began walking down the hall with me. "What's your spike size? There's only two weeks until —"

"Hey, coach?"

"Yeah?" His Adam's apple mercurying up and down in anticipation.

"Want to see me run?" And I was gone before the answer, skidding between backpacks and cliques, not stopping till I made it home. I am fast, I remember thinking. So what?

So this, I thought. Good to be fast when you can honor your commitment to only running when someone's chasing. This ought to be easy. And it was. My body took on a sort of senselessness, where I couldn't even feel my edges anymore, just the rumor of where I was and the fact that I was approaching.

I ran in a straight line, sweat down my temple like oil for my engine. My feet were not touching the ground but skimming over it, surfing the surface but never sinking. The quiet pulse of my heart became all I heard. The enemy and their chorus of war were far behind and not worth fearing. I had the faith that I could truly run all the way home. Past the hotel, whether it was still standing or not. Past the meeting point of my kidnapping. Past my old school where the track coach would still be timing sluggards in mesh shirts and have to stop to watch me blow by him like an unmade promise.

My tongue dried but not from fatigue. My mouth had planked open from the, yes, joy of it all. The speed, the getaway, the privacy. This is me, I thought. This is what I do. I don't stay and wait and worry. I react and move. I get gone. My entire life had been a slow vanishing act. I could do this. I could run until my molecules became one with the filthy air. And all the dirty gray of my soul, propelled at the proper speed, would allow me, once and for all, to disappear. I could feel it happening now. My flesh coming off or the air gluing onto this shape that I carried around. Space began to wrap itself around me. Every jut and joint, from cheekbones to Achilles tendon. Every neuron and proton was sealing into place. Invisible. Invisible. A little, only just a little faster and then invisible.

My mouth closed. My lungs and heart became one. All I had left to do was close my eyes so that I would be the last one to ever see me. But I couldn't. Not yet. There was something else I needed to see before. A thousand soldiers.

No, fewer. But soldiers, still. Moving. Toward me. For a moment I thought I had been running the wrong way. But these were not my tower-view soldiers. These men moved in an accidental weave. They held hatchets and hammers, knives and broken guns. They weren't really soldiers at all but citizens. Survivors. A militia born of skin-to-the-bone need. They weren't running from but toward. They wanted the thousand soldiers behind me, and they had no choice but to think I was the scout. That I was the first one on the scene. That I had done this to their land.

With only fifty yards between their onslaught and my ignorant explanation, there would be no time for diplomacy. They would slice me sideways like the horse and rush on to their own death. For, despite their fervor and fury, it wouldn't take many bullets and grenades to turn this street into their cemetery.

"I'm sorry," I said, not stopping to explain, not having the luxury to warn. Besides, they wanted what was coming. They chose to die this way.

I maintained my speed but looked left and right. Forward and backward had ceased to be options. Memory told me I had come from the left, that my border there was the sea. So I angled right and sprinted on, even as a machete pierced the path my foot had just trod. I heard the far grumble of their language. Was it the same as on the radio show? Or was it just anger pitched at such a volume that it was its own tongue? I ran on, untired and unknown. Ran until there was silence again. Except for the distant thrash and gunfire of the tribes being culled down to one.

The train car shouldn't have been there either. Like the horse. The electrical tower belonged in the remains of this city as a sign of former connections. Of the darkness that follows all the bright lights of war. But the horse, and now this silver-black commuter car lying on its side like a metal Labrador, had seemed to bubble up from the stew the violence was stirring.

There were no train tracks. Certainly not visible ones. And there were no other cars, hitched or unhitched. This was neither an engine nor a caboose. It was a middle child in whatever family had been pulling it, and now it was as orphaned as I was under the slow fall of the noonday sky.

I was glad for it, that much was certain. It was an enclosed refuge and housed at least the possibility of rest for my suddenly pain-encased feet. I didn't know how far I had gone on my dash, but the blisters and twinges below my ankles said that I had gone far enough.

I stepped up onto its metal steps, expecting the door to slide open for me. Instead, the mirrored glass failed to show me my reflection or open. I imagined the far-off sound of the violent tribes approaching to motivate the strength I would need to get inside. Two elbow jabs to the glass broke only my elbow, or nearly. I jammed my fingers into the thin

space between metal and rubber, using them as tiny crow-
bars, until they almost snapped off too. Some hiding place. I
couldn't even get inside.

I stepped back down and quickly circled the train like a
man in a hurry to buy a used car. The outside didn't promise
much of an interior. It looked like a workaday commuter
line, silver as an old filling, graffitied like a high-school
kid's backpack or, in more recent time, like a high-school
kid's skin. All the way around I hustled until I could see that
the roof had a hatch. It had been damaged in whatever
mishap had befallen this vehicle, and its mangled orifice was
aimed at the sun. It caught just enough light to reflect an
invitation.

A running start propelled me up off the top step to just
the bottom lip of the roof. I pulled it down nearly into a
frown as I armed and legged it up and over. The hatch had
been crushed open, but not wide enough for a man. I
needed leverage, but I was too tired to provide my own, so
I leaned against the slim opening and gave up. For a while I
pretended that giving up had been the whole damn point.
That this entrance was the type that only yielded to a coded
touch, a gentle knock, never panicked force. The small of
my back would simply need to apply the perfect percent-
age of pressure, and the entire hatch would open wide as a
lion's mouth, and I would be swallowed into a softer, safer
world. No.

Then I recalled a cartoon I had seen as a child where a man kept encountering wall after wall on his morning walk. It seemed profoundly unjust, even in my early youth, that this innocent lank should be forced to scramble over one impractical wall after another. He wasn't training for an event. He wasn't escaping a prison. He was just trying to go for a goddamn walk. But still the walls came, each higher than the last, and each scaled by his relentless optimism and dwindling strength. Until he dared to be happy. Dared to celebrate the scaling of one particular wall. For soon his punishment would be the highest wall of all. So he gave up. I still remember vividly how I'd clapped for him at that moment. Out loud in the theater, confusing my brother into clapping along, to which he'd added a couple of woo-hoos. Yet I wasn't clapping encouragement. I was clapping his decision to end his walk. Fucking walls, enough of you. Sit down, attaboy. Have a rest. I turned to my mother and said, "Good."

"Shhh," she gently breathed. "It's not over."

"Over!" my little brother exclaimed, clapping again, but directly in front of his nose like an organ grinder's monkey. Sadly, she was right. It wasn't over. My long-legged friend stood up. And instead of walking back home for a little cold soda and a change of shoes, he started, the stupid son of a bitch, to climb the wall. "No," I protested. "That's not the way it . . . the way it needs to end."

"You tell that," my mother said, leading us by the hand out of the theater like a butcher carrying slippery chickens, "to the animator the next time you see him." The credits were rolling as I yanked a peek back at the screen. The words moving fast and meaningless upon its shimmering blackness.

"That's not fair," I said, still turned toward the screen.

"Two movies and a cartoon seems OK fair to me. How about you, nubbin?" She asked my blissful baby brother for backup, and he provided it with a spectacularly grateful smile. But I wasn't sad we were leaving. I was sad that the poor schmuck kept climbing. Hadn't he learned what was on the other side of that wall?

So on the top of the train car, I decided to really give up. Because even if I did crank open the hatch with adrenalized strength, there would only be another hatch or door or lock to jimmy or pick or explode. No, I was going to give up. If for no other reason than to see what happens when you really surrender.

"I give up," I announced. My voice bounced off the metal like a flat snore. I liked the way it sounded coming out of my mouth. Ironically confident. Shyly sure. I. Give. Up.

"No, you don't," she said. "Not this time." The hatch began to open. From the inside.

It had been probably seven years, but she looked almost identical. Her hair was shorter, so I knew she had become a

mother, and the skin around her eyes had grown more transparent with time. A tiny blue vein pulsed just beneath the
surface of one. She backed down the small ladder that led inside the train. She even kept a hand on my leg as I dropped
down in. We were in the dining car. It wasn't a commuter.
Tables replaced regular seating and the galley was visible behind her, halfway down the car.

"They said you might come," she said. "I wasn't sure how
long to wait." I was too undone by her face to ask who or
why. The dent at the top of her nose. The dust of freckles
cinnamoning across her left cheek. Her neck long and white
as a candle, with her lovely face the flame. "You're shaking,"
she worried, and guided me toward one of the dining tables.
The chairs were molded plastic, but they felt like the deepest leather as I sat myself down.

"I'm cold," I lied. These were the shakes of shame. Of
corruption. Of walking into a church when I should have
been walking into a prison. Of how much I had disappointed
her but far more how deeply I had disappointed myself. Who
walks away from this (I scraped the question across my brain
to dig the deepest trenches) and chooses war? I wanted to be
nineteen in the sugar-sweet rain and dumb in love again.
Not ruined and useless, the object of pity. I was shaking so
fast because I was desperately trying to shed my skin.

"It's warm in here," she offered, instead of her coat or an
embrace. "You'll feel better."

I wasn't sure if she used only words because she didn't want to be too near to me or she trusted they would be enough. "W-w-what are you doing?" I chattered through clicked teeth. "Here?"

"I was sent. I was asked for." Her tone gave away no surprise, neither at the request nor the reality.

"They said, 'Come meet him? He's in a train?' "

"*On* a train."

"You're still funnier than I am," I said.

"Everyone's funnier than you. It was one of my favorite things. If I could make you laugh . . ." And she let out a hopeful breath that seemed to bloom as it traveled. By the time it hit my ears, it tickled.

"Now I'm laughing and shaking," I said, "like a lunatic."

"Lunatics are all right." She smiled, her fingers playing an invisible chord on the tabletop. "At least they love one thing . . . with everything."

"But the moon can't love them back," I ricocheted.

"Then I guess I was the lunatic." The weight of memory bowed her head. We were quiet for a while. I eyed the empty train. It seemed possible we could ride things out here inside this useless hunk of steel. If there was food, she wouldn't have to go back. To wherever she now belonged, with whomever had brought her.

"I missed my life," I said. "I came out here to kill and all I've wanted to do is die. And even that I can't get done. I missed my whole life." She didn't look up, but her shoulders gave away that she was crying. "I'm sorry. I'm sorry I kidnapped you. Should've just let you be."

"No."

"OK," I allowed. "Thanks."

"I'm all right now. A little boy. And girl. Bangs. Cowlicks. Days full of playgrounds. I'm all right."

"Good," I said, and I meant it. I also noticed that I'd stopped shaking. "Husband, I guess." Biting down hard to keep my voice from cracking.

"Yes."

"Not a lunatic, right?" I said to my impossibly, imperfectly beautiful ex-wife. "I bet he knows how to love many things." She exhaled her yes, stretched out her hand and almost touched me.

"Look at you. You're . . ."

"War," I said. "At least now the inside and the outside match." She rose as quickly as a bird scared from a branch, quick-stepped to the galley, and began searching for something amid the crooked shelves and smashed glass. I peered out the window to the clatter of her investigation. Outside the tribes collided.

Using blade and barrel, they slaughtered each other. Bone into bone and blood in the air like an afterthought. I crossed the aisle to watch the carnage from my trackless sanctuary. The war was old now, or old enough to unleash final weapons. Arrows, Molotovs, chains to necklace a man to death. Bodies fell like drunks until it was impossible to decipher who was finishing whom. Then a noise. A wail like a trumpet blast, an air-raid horn, but one born inside the head.

I slammed my palms over my ears for protection, and still they ached like tetanus. My ex steadied herself against the aural assault, words streaming from her mouth, all unheard. The soldiers outside fled, or covered themselves in bodies first and then crawled out and fled this plague of noise. Just as I dared to shout against it, it fell as if from a cliff and splashed down without a sound.

I hustled to her side, and we fell into seats, shaking our heads and rubbing our jaws. "Ouch," she said. "What was that?"

"Loud," I said. "That was loud."

"Uh-oh. You were just funny."

I laughed. I laughed like a kid who knew what was in the box before even shaking it. Like an old man who finally catches the fish of a lifetime and there is no one around to show. Oh yeah, and he's a notorious liar, so he knows no one will believe. Yes. I laughed like that. Then she laughed, and I even louder, until we were laughing only to not have to stop laughing, to not have to face the silent car, the ruined corpses, the mad impossibility of this fractured, gorgeous interlude.

"We shouldn't stay," I finally said. "They'll come back to collect their dead and . . ."

"I know."

"What are you looking for?" As answer she set up on the table a roll of paper towels, a bottle of water, and a bar of soap, blue as menthol and stronger in scent. "You want me to clean the place up before we go?" I laughed again, this one sad. "I don't think the next renters will be by for a couple of generations." I finished the joke slowly, knowing that good-byes were on the other side of it. My throat clotted with years of noes. Of anger and pressure and grief the size of the globe. I swigged the water, but most of it fought its way back up.

"I have to go," she said. Tears tricked the seal of my eyelashes as she handed me the towels and soap. "I can't do this for you." She wept. "But please . . ." Her face on my cheek left the gentlest scar. "Wash as if I am."

I went straight to work, peeling off my clothes like a beech tree hungry for clean winter. With my boots unstuck, my soles tingled electric on the train-car floor. Naked, I doused the soap with water and lathered up a sudden foam. I did the first arm in a hurry, then allowed her request to take root. My hands eased, my muscles uncramped, and I, slowly and as close to tenderly as I could get, washed myself clean.

The soap rivered through the blood and mud cake of my wound. I pushed in with a necessary pain and sent thank-you to my hawk for how he'd guaranteed I still had a limb to cleanse. I washed my feet, between the toes, bruxed the soap over my heels until they were slippery enough to skate on.

I took my time, picturing my ex doing my back as I un-stuck inches of grit and battle dust. I rubbed my neck like a kiss and remembered the last one we'd ever had. In a drive-way. She, off to work, not knowing. I, waiting for her tail-lights to vanish so I could coward away. Only this time the kiss was good and safe. This time the kiss wasn't the last, it was the first.

I said her name while I washed my hair, then used nearly all the water to rinse myself done. Standing in inches of filthy water, the suds brown between my toes, I stepped clear and doused my feet with what remained. I was wet and new as a summer baby. I didn't want to look up because I knew she would be gone.

"Your face," she said from the far doorway. I could see only her back, her shyness another precious gem in her crown.

"You can't go that way," I told her, even as the metal door slid open at her touch.

"You forgot." Only her voice now. "Your face."

"I didn't forget," I said, touching the place her hand had been. Feeling that, beneath the grime, it was already clean.

The door closed after she vanished. And I stood there trembling, dripping, waiting for her to have left. Instead, the shivers returned. I dressed, yanking stiff clothes over new, cool skin. Boots last, and I was a soldier again, or at least I looked like one. All dressed up and nowhere to run.

"————." It was her full name. It sounded like the answer to a question. "I don't give up." The longest silence. Nothing. Just me, bathed, alive in the food car. That was when I should have been laughing. I looked up at the hatch I had climbed through and took aim. It was still open the same original sliver, and it would not give an inch. Shoulders, back, legs, all forcing. Nothing. *FUCK!* I wanted to say. Instead, against my will, I repeated, "I don't give up."

"Good," she said. And with my left hand I lifted the hatch, climbed out onto the roof of the train. The sun had found a hammock in the horizon, and the late light seemed to melt the place where I was standing. I started walking. My feet even felt better. Walking away from the scattered bodies and my hideaway train. Faster, and I was thinking, I know what I said to my ex back there, but please, somebody, whoever . . . No more walls.

"But you said," my ex reminded me. Immediately.

"OK, OK. Walls. Bring on the fucking walls."

The sky was dragon-skin blue as night chased day like a monster. But somehow on this evening it didn't seem dark out at all. The atmosphere had a sheen to it, the air above filled with refulgent light.

Was I in Jerusalem, walking an ancient road, now destroyed by Armageddon? I didn't have the Sunday-school knowledge to faithfully answer the question, but I did remember the mention of wars and rumors of wars. Had it all come so quickly? Perhaps I was walking toward the Holy City and would encounter a berobed and bearded original who could pencil in the gaps. Maybe there'd be a star to guide me, the idiot shepherd with nothing better to do than leave his flock and go searching for the King.

I suddenly felt that, being faithless, I lacked a piece of armor or, at the very least, a map. A rudimentary understanding of the possibilities. How could I know it was the end of the world without having paid any attention during the end-of-the-world discussions? It seemed both unfair and absolutely deserved.

The fact was, my life had prepared me for nothing. I had never learned to enjoy things. To treasure people or circumstances. I had calendared from one anger to the next. My years before the hotel had prepared me for one thing. To kill. The death of my brother should have made me spurn mortality, long for life and its discontents. Instead I'd romanticized and romanced death. I sniffed it out like an airport dog. I'd arrayed myself in the glamour of it so that, by the time I said yes to these assholes, there was no life in me. I was unconscious and conscience-free. I was eager to obey and find direction in my directionless life. Let me point my fury. Point, aim, and fire. They gave us dog tags not to identify the living but to separate the dead.

I tried to make a list as I walked of all the things I had wanted to do with my life. I didn't need a pen because there was nothing to write down. Perhaps I could make a few up. Senator. Album-cover designer. Cooper. Bartender. Short-order cook. Street-corner evangelist. Tugboat captain. Ball-hog soccer player. Mediocre cellist. Detective first grade.

But these weren't identities, they were jobs. Was I my father's son? My mother's worry? My brother's keeper? Failed on that account. Was it the true me who asked the ice cream girl to marry me, or was it me in the driveway, kissing her off and gone? Don't say both. I did both, yes, but only one could be true. I didn't want to be split in half. If I was shit, let me be shit till it's all shit and I could blend in. Or let me be light. Dare I even say it? I didn't want to dream I could be like my ex, like my brother, even my mother, because then I might want to live, and the landscape in front of me was still looking like a cemetery without tombs.

I stepped on something big as my foot, and it crumbled beneath my weight like a beached horseshoe crab. I didn't stop to see if it was a human forearm. I was thinking too much, examining, trying to understand. I could have saved time by lighting a flare and sticking it in my mouth to help the enemy end my too-long night.

But the question remained . . . Who was my enemy? I'd watched the tribes pierce each other through as if they enjoyed it, yet I'd recognized nothing but the color of their blood. That, we all shared. Bright red, then back in the air and on the ground. When we went we only knew how to paint one picture. Maybe it didn't matter anymore.

War is a cycle of viciousness and revenge that never ends. A Möbius strip of mayhem and misunderstanding that generates only burials and insurrection. And yet, for all the emptiness and futility, I still found myself yearning to be somewhere. Comprehending something. Even if the news turned out to be all bad, I continued to search the dial. Not out of hope. Out of necessity. Because as long as limbs, brain, and heart were working, I seemed utterly incapable of lying down and dying.

Up ahead, what had to be a line of trees looked like a dead heat of galloping horses. The bright-blue light of the evening was vanishing as they ran from the approaching tsunami of darkness. It came so fast, there wasn't time to prepare for the blackout. An eclipse? That felt biblical, too. But there hadn't been a moon visible to eclipse since I'd arrived. I sat down to wait it out. The ground around me was soft to the touch, with the give of hot fudge, and it took every effort to keep me from shoveling a fistful into my mouth. My stomach pinched itself tighter in obedience, and I waited for the eclipse to pass. It did not. I lay down. This is not lying down and dying, I reminded myself. This is just lying down.

The scream woke me up. It was the same siren my ex and I had heard, the eardrum liquidator, the wave of sound playing across my ribs like a xylophone. It was also bright morning. I had slept a needed sleep, and I peeled myself up from the imprint I'd left in the mud.

The horse trees were gone, and there was nothing visible in any direction, but the sound seemed close enough to be howling from within my head.

"Excuse me," the man said, the sound vanishing at the sound of his voice. His ability to sneak up behind me could only be attributed to the veil of sound. It had been so loud, even sight was vibrated to static. "You shouldn't be here. This isn't safe. Or have you lost your battalion?" He had the gray pallor of a failed insurance investigator. His suit was tattered and plucked, and a line of blood ran from each ear.

"Yes," I answered. "I am lost."

His answer came as if he'd heard me, but I knew it impossible. It's just that his advice matched up with my need.

"Get underground. They're going to bring the hammer down next."

"What hammer?"

"And that will be it. There's nothing after that. There's barely something before it."

His siren was chipped-red, with a mouth like a cowbell and a hand crank thick as a rolling pin. "World War II?"

"I've been ringing since this started. Now there's no one around to listen." We both looked back, and I saw that I had walked through another battlefield. "You were supposed to protect us."

Deafness made his accent difficult to discern. "Who? Protect who? We were sent to fight."

"Too much fighting," he said, gazing out to the horizon where my horse trees reappeared. "Not enough saving." I wanted to ask him to take me with him. But the promise of permanent deafness and his vacant look meant we would have been vulnerable partners. He reached for the crank again, but I stopped him. His arm was strong, and his red-black eyes said let go.

"Wait. You said 'underground.' Where can I go underground?" He kept straining for the crank as if my stopping him was costing lives per second. I pointed forcefully to the earth. "Underground. Tell me."

"Too late," he said. "They'll find you now." I let his arm go, and he split the air with sonic pain. I had no choice but to run. Just like my trees, which were now not neck-and-neck. They were five deep, scattered yet tight, and they were fifty feet from trampling me down.

They were riderless yet not wild. Each wore a saddle and works, save one that had spit the bit and was gnashing at the air as if the oxygen were made of sugar. They'd escaped from a stable, or lost their riders to bullets, and the siren was making them insane. Faster and madder, they spirited toward me, while the siren was making me gnash at the air, too. I three-quarters ran, ears covered, but the horses gained on me. Get away, I thought. Getaway. The palomino was the ugliest, but it was the lead horse and seemed most in a hurry. I slowed my jaunt and covered my ears as long as possible.

My left hand caught the rein with such a jerk that it pulled his head a full ninety and locked my elbow like a safe. My heels dug into the soft turf and the animal slowed just enough for me to camp-climb up his hinds and into the saddle in one satisfying slide. Then he ran on like I'd never even joined him. He led his group farther and farther from the old man and his warning. And even though we rode for miles, lost the other ponies and found enough gap for comfort, we could both still hear the moment that he took his hand off the crank.

Thirst. That's what caused the horse to gallop to the small eddy of water about thirty yards away. His energy had come suddenly after an hour of exhausted tiptoeing. He had run out of three of his shoes and his hooves were blood-splashed. Each step elicited a thin whinny of pain, and he shook his mane in hopes of dislodging the enormous fly on his back. I dismounted and dropped to my knees, lapping with both hands, letting it make a flag down the front of my shirt.

The horse drank, then dipped its sore feet into the water. It didn't work, so he dropped to his forelegs to ease the pressure. Within seconds he was on his side. I finished slaking, then went to him, stroked the glorious neck, the salt stains thick as paint. His long lashes tickled the water. His breathing faded to a tiny low rumble. I leaned against him, unsentimentally, then struggled not to cry. Nothing's getting out alive. No one. I even imagined digging a grave for the bastard because I was tired of not having a job to do. He fixed that dilemma by sitting bolt upright, knocking me sideways into the water. He got to his feet gingerly, but once up he tightened his shoulders, shook his fierce head at me, and trotted off.

"All right," I exclaimed. Happy for the horse until I realized I'd just lost my ride, although it wouldn't be needed. I was going to stay there for a while. Turned out there *was* a grave that needed to be dug.

Just a little farther down, in the direction the horse had vacated, was the body. The drenched uniform still bore our flag, and the boots were the same as mine. But it wasn't until I stood over the body that I knew I'd be burying R. The gloss of his skin betrayed that he'd been dead since the day I lost him after our water crossing. But he'd been in the water most of the time, until he'd washed up on the small patch of earth, so the birds hadn't been at him.

I used the butt of his gun to dig the first inches down but needed more leverage and width. I slit open his SAPI and removed the now-pointless bulletproof porcelain plates from the front and back. They did what they could during his life. Now they would dig him his shelter in death. It took well into the day, with the regular water breaks and the times I'd just sit next to R. and tell him stories. Told him about all the shit we talked about him at the hotel. (That was a lie. We didn't have enough camaraderie as soldiers to truly pick out a target for personal attacks.) I told him all the lies I could remember from my youth. The shark-killing lies from elementary school. The "that dent was there when I got back to the car" lies I'd told my dad. The lies I'd told women in bars to make them go away: How I'd lost a foot on an oil rig. How my teeth were all soldered together after a boating accident. How I was so afraid of the dark, if the lights ever went out, I'd been known to burn down the house. R. laughed. Or I imagined he laughed. They weren't great stories, but they were mine, and it was good to look back and see how ridiculous I had been. How it might be nice to have a chance to make some new stories. Live them, not lie them. The longer I talked to R., the better I felt. It was turning into the best funeral I'd ever attended.

I traded uniforms with R. We were about the same size and mine was dry. He'd been souping in his own gear long enough. He deserved, if not a proper dress burial, then at least a better-dressed burial. I kept my boots. Every man had the right to die in his own boots.

With the sun small as a tangerine, peeking through the clouds, I gently rolled R. into his grave.

I stood at attention and saluted him for the first time since I'd been under his command. "Good night, sir." I began with two handfuls of dirt. "God bless, then. I guess. God bless."

Strangely, it took longer to fill than to empty the grave, and I found my will and body growing weaker. The first part had seemed like a favor, a way to honor a fallen comrade. The second just felt like covering a corpse with dirt, and I didn't like it. I needed a bigger tool to shift earth. I scuffled about, kicking at the edge of things until something would be willing to stick its neck out. My boot finally made contact with the end of a metal pole.

I knew it would be useless in the service of speeding R.'s burial, but I also knew by its shape, length, and material that it wasn't any old metal pole. It was the bottom of a street sign that had been buried upside down in the tumult. And since I was looking at the ass end, buried about three feet deeper, with any luck, would be the name of a street. In a language I could possibly understand. I sensed I was about three feet from knowing where I was.

But first, I had to finish my soldier's duty, and if I knew where I was at last, I mightn't have had the stamina for the grave job at hand. I dug and dug in other areas to create enough cover for R. to rest in peace. The energy was back and I bulldozed piles of dirt like I had an engine and tires. Sweat stung from every pore, salted my eyes, fed my lips. I was a euphoric undertaker, and with a final shouldered shove it was done. I stuck his gun (sans bullets) in the ground, crossed myself like a superstitious shortstop, and slowly walked back to the metal pole.

I yanked it like bad wisdom from the street's dirty mouth and fell back laughing. On my knees I crawled to the top of the sign and it was there. Covered in inches of muck, but the metal rectangle that would announce my location was in my hands.

I splashed into the water and scraped and clawed at the tumbling mud. The words came out in cipher, the letters separated by commas of dirt. Almost, soldier, I told myself. You're just about to know.

Some things in life you know before you know them. They say some cancer patients know long before diagnosis that something is growing inside of them. Long before tests show even the slightest malformation. Likewise they know they are healed, if so lucky, and are known for telling their doctors the good news before the machines and science of it all confirms their faith. I didn't know before I began washing the street sign. I truly had no idea whether it would read Al-Sadr Blvd. or bear the markings of the Sudanese rebels. But once I saw the C, once I felt the rough surface of the engraving, I knew there was only one word beneath the fury and the filth. And that word was VICTORY.

What is man's place in the world? Is it enough to never know why? Simply that we are alive and that we have a responsibility to want to remain that way? If death is the denial of the one thing in life we are sure of — that we are here — then war must be man's desire to deny that God ever made us at all.

Staring at the street sign in my hand, with the block number etched into the bottom right corner, I felt as if I had never lived. As if every detail in my life had been the ingredients of a design never manufactured. That I had been a bad idea, dismissed before egg ever met sperm. My stomach boomeranged its own emptiness into a cramp that forced me to drop the sign and stand up so straight and quick it was as if I was being summoned for punishment. Everything receded like spent dreams, and I stood at the center of my discovery, Columbus at the edge of a flat world.

If the sign had been buried where it originally stood, then I was less than half a block from my house. I swayed in hopes of not having to move my feet. To trick my memory into the idea that I was too crippled to walk. But my knee bent, foot lifted, and I began the journey to 714 Victory Lane. With each step, the war seemed to peel back like old wallpaper, and the street of my youth appeared beneath.

Mr. Z.'s rose bushes thorned across my vision, a cartoon of color and fragrance. I could hear his spaniel skating over kitchen tiles to reach the door and bark at my arrival.

The next house was red and white as a firehouse, and the widow D. and her three sons emergencied out of the driveway, always late for something. Her hair was wet with hurry, and the boys blamed each other, then fell into laughter as the car raced by, almost clipping my toes.

My wounded stiffness began to yield to a common calm. I knew how to walk on this street, even if it was only memories and detritus now. I finally knew where I was; the shock and the comfort creating a weird nausea. I felt both sick and healed at the same time.

Mr. and Mrs. G. were out on their front porch. She held an iced-tea glass so slick with condensation it seemed to be melting in her hand. Her husband's smile and wave were borrowed from an advertisement. A version of happiness, well lit, organized, and utterly false. She dropped the glass, and at the shatter their house was gone.

Five more houses, I thought, until I reached home. And I suddenly became terrified of who I would find there.

Would it include my father, his belly Santa-Claused with cancer, a lit cigarette in his mouth, a dying man's final flare? Would little brother be running in stitches at my mother's feet, like a shredded rag doll sewn together by the sickness of nostalgia? And would Mom be watching and worrying, still as a Rockwell painting, her eyes reaching out but her arms and feet doing nothing to greet me?

I walked on.

Past the Spanish family's house, where the open kitchen window leaked the scent of tonight's dinner like a badly kept secret. I could see Señora in her apron and sleeveless T-shirt, stirring something so fast her shoulders gleamed like shined copper.

Next came the St. famille, Canadians who had daughters big as sons. Their garage door was kissed black from all the street hockey it had witnessed face first. The girls practiced hard moves on their own, while the father, his thighs almost alien-wide, singsonged his way through his athletic advice. He waved to me, too, sincere but rushed, with the promise of a later chat in its bright force.

"You're dead," I told him. "This is our only chance to talk." But he smiled with chaw-stained teeth and shrugged. As if even death couldn't flatten those thighs, his will, his yes.

Across the street a white stucco house, shutters as black as mascaraed eyes, stood empty and bold. I tried to recall who'd lived there, but the mailbox name slot was as empty as it had always been. That was the house that had been owned and caretaken but never occupied. Like an orphan who remained unadopted. It looked perfect, ready for life to spring out of its door. And yet it was empty. Some things never get a chance to fill their space in the world. It was dust and dirt now. Maybe that was what it had always longed to be.

I could hear my brother then. He was in the yard, but what he was saying or doing was still just beyond reach. I looked to our nearest neighbor instead and let little brother's volume be the final guide in.

The neighbor's place was in the process of being painted. Mr. F. was halfway up a ladder with a fresh bucket of the pale yellow that was glistening wet in the equally pale sunlight. I could tell his back hurt as he limped up the rungs. His two sons had long been married and on the other coast, and his resentment was visible in every stutter step and audible in each mumbled curse.

"Looks great," I yelled.

"Yep." That's all he said. Didn't turn around. Didn't ask for help. Just accepted that the work was his to complete and he was doing a damn fine job at it. "No one's home." This he said passively, as if his disappointment in his boys had become acceptance.

"Do you want a hand?" I asked, trying but failing to walk toward him.

"I mean for you, son. No one's home." And he was gone. It was all gone, reduced to the vast void the war had damned it to. All gone except for me. In front of my house. And no one was home.

My brother's voice had ceased. The lights were all off. And even in the quasidaylight of hallucination, the house seemed dark and uninviting. "Hell." I bothered. Then, without walking, I was at the front door. The house had slid up to meet me, and there was only going in.

The foyer was cool as a greenhouse. I closed the door, and the house began. Brother ghosting past me in a dark blur of hurry and worry. "Help," he was saying, or "Need help." Then up the stairs as if vacuumed away. Mother in the dining room, setting the table for four, then three, then two, then one. The silverware quivered back into her hand, she began again.

"You're back," my dad said from the living room. He was in his bottle-green hospital gown and his eyes were so red and wounded he appeared to be in the process of getting beaten up.

"I never left," I countered. I didn't want him to be able to make any statement of fact about me. "And you're dead."

"Sure I am, boy. But that doesn't mean you didn't ass your way back." Gone. Fast as the smoke that had killed him.

I climbed the stairs with teenage agility and stood in my bedroom like a stunned thief. Man, that was easy. Now, what do I take? There were no trophies or graduation tassels. No favorite books or CD collection. There was very little to determine a boy ever lived here, ever battled the sheets for a soft enough place to sleep. Ever listened for monsters or wished that they'd come. Ever kissed my ex for the first time, her tender bottom blessing the edge of my mattress.

Brother's room was locked. Took a broad soldier's shoulder to splinter the tiny lock. Inside were all my things. My canvases, paints, and brushes. Even the one I'd destroyed. My clothes were in here, too. Sneakers I wore to outrace the track star. Even a news clipping I'd torn from the local paper about the track star's record-breaking time. There were letters, too. From my ex, her father, even her friends, all asking me why and why not return. She's waiting. She has forgiveness in her heart. It wasn't the first time I had read them.

I lay down on my little brother's bed, my feet dangling over like a giant's. I wasn't tired. I was just hoping to remember what it felt like to be small.

"It's no fun," he said in the doorway. "Not if you stay this way." I turned to sit up but was pinned with such fatigue, even turning onto my side took yeoman's effort. "Need help," I heard him say again, and tears fell down my face sideways.

"I'm sorry," I confessed. "Sorry I wasn't there. To catch

you, or push you. Whatever it was." Little brother blurred in and out, between my tears and his sudden proximity. He was standing over me, brushing salt away with his crooked fingers.

"You didn't hear me," he said, whispering my name. "I said, 'Do you need help?'"

"Yes."

The word fell out like an atom and split the world into a trillion pieces. Brother, mother, father, house, neighbors, Victory, all subsided in a single, explosive word. Yes.

No one was there to hear it, so I said it again to make certain. "Yes," I murmured. Then shouted, then sang, then spoke. "Yes."

I was alone, yet not alone. As I rose from the cool of the soil that had played the part of my little brother's bed, all the emptiness around me became crowded at the edges. Their hands brushed the mud from my cheek, painted my tears down my face with their fingers. They adjusted my posture and turned me in a direction. Then they waited for me to lead.

I didn't need to see their faces to know who they were. To detective out their aromas or the cut of their clothes to be able to say hello. They knew me. I knew them. That was enough. What was clear was that they expected me to walk and they would follow. I began to protest the redundancy of my lostness, but they silenced me with their faith. They believed I knew which direction to head. And that gave me enough strength to begin the journey.

This was Victory Lane. But it wasn't my Victory. It was another street that had once been thick with barbecuing neighbors and lost baseballs in the yard. A street like ten thousand before it and others yet to come, where people dig down deep, as if the wind will never blow hard enough. But war had finally visited. It traveled as it always has, inexorably, without prejudice, uprooting every inch of the planet and daring the survivors to rebuild. They will, and it will return. The cycle will never finish, I thought.

I began to wish I was in a place that deserved war. Places where the images of mustached leaders were held aloft by fanatic murderers. Cities where demand outstripped supply so that only thievery would buy justice. Vast, open deserts where tribal aim met tribal target and generators bled uselessly into the sand, until the earth itself was a wound, and there was nothing worth saving.

Or a cold place where nuclear winter existed even before the bomb. Why not a crowded Asian street, filthy with slavery and yearning, that needed a fresh beginning, a zeroing out. Yet no place deserved war. All cities, towns, villages had once been bucolic and serene. Every house had at least a sliver of hope before being blown to smithereens.

I had volunteered for a fight without caring who I was fighting. I was eager only for self-negation and the erasure of other selves along the way, be they enemy or even Y., with his broken windpipe and flailing impotence back at the hotel bar. I'd wanted to burn things down. I'd longed not just to be in a war but to become war. Itself.

Even as a teenager, I'd thought the refugees of war were lucky to be leaving. They could begin again, away from death. But death has speed and greed in its loins, and pursuit is its favorite game. It allows us to escape because it knows where we live. And death is patient because it knows if it doesn't come to us, we will surely come to it.

Even the peacekeepers, like my Dutch wallflower, didn't know who they were supposed to protect. That this was sacred land made of families and futures. Picnics and popcorn. Sweaters in the winter and sunburns in July. This was a real place, once, and it deserved protection. Attention. Someone guarding the gate. I had been hired as a soldier, paid well, fed and liquored, lied to and manipulated. But I was still a soldier and I was still alive.

And this final walk wasn't about death. It was about life. That's what my mother said, without speaking. She was just to my left, her hair tousled gray the way it had been when I found her breathless in her bed three days before I decided to go to war. She had invited me over the way she often did, with the promise of a cake and lemonade. On the few occasions that I'd accepted the invite, I'd always stopped at the corner store to get the supplies. We'd bake together, laughing and looking out the window, letting our proximity be an embrace. Then we'd drink the lemonade while the cake cooled, and I would always leave without a taste.

But on that day — with the oven preheated and an empty pitcher (its mouth awaiting sweet powder) standing guard by the sink — I'd climbed the steps calling her name, already sensing she wouldn't need it anymore. Kissed her forehead. Massaged her arthritic knuckles, her hands still warm. "Nothing left," I'd said, and I shed the final skin of what I thought was my life.

But this one had different wisdom. This time Mom was saying that no matter what you think you leave behind, until your heart stops, you carry it all with you. Everything. And everyone. Little brother agreed. He took my hand and forced me to keep up the pace. "We'll lose the others," I said.

"No, we won't." One look back told me he was right again. There was my ex, her face bright as a Polaroid flash. She walked with confidence and grace. I could see she believed I was moving in the right direction.

O. was behind her, his face hazier, but still held captive by a smile. His father was standing by his side. I knew little brother had my hand, was my rudder, so I kept looking back into the group who trailed behind. "Is it everyone?" I asked my brother.

"Not everyone."

R. came into focus, as if I'd never laid him in the ground. His ruined eye seemed to heal long enough to see me, then collapsed again. But that wasn't healing, it was his hello. I laughed. "Where are we going?" I asked him, as I had a hundred times under his command.

"You know, soldier. Walk on." Seeing R. made me strain to find Mc., but like brother had said, this train did not hold everyone.

My sniper. He came into focus just beside R. He had the floating gait of a skater, his effort effortless. The filth had gone from his face, and by his clothes and shoes I could guess that he was an American, just like me. Nineteen, tops. Maybe he'd spared my life because he couldn't bear to shoot the mirror. But it had cost him his. Why was he trusting me to lead the way across this humming horizon of flattened light?

"Over here," little brother insisted, and I turned back around in time to see the man who'd died along with him. The car-crash driver and his grief-sick son. They darted in and out of my periphery as if trying to enter the busy flow of traffic. "Let them in." I slowed, and the father and son eased in just past my left shoulder. They seemed relieved. In rhythm.

I went to speak but saw my hero instead. The one who'd dragged me to safety on the battlefield and lost his life in the pull. He was dressed in jeans and a pale yellow shirt that had fit him as a college kid and fit him still. He flashed a grin, and thank-yous fell out like broken teeth. "Don't thank me," I complained.

"Hush now," little brother said. "He's teaching. He was a teacher before this. Still teaching." And as I watched more closely, the thank-yous became birds that fell from the cage of his mouth and winged forward so fast, it turned me back around to face front. Still walking. Still no destination in sight.

"Tell us a story," my dead prisoners requested. It was all of them, suddenly walking in front of, beside, and behind me. They moved between the others without anyone noticing. Their skin was transparent and dark as sea stones, and hands were pressed together gently, so as not to crack the secret they were keeping.

"You tell me." I turned the tables.

"But, ————," they said my name in unison, "we already have."

Look up. Look up and see where you are standing. I couldn't tell if it was me chiding myself, or little brother with one more instruction. It didn't matter. I looked up. And saw. I was standing in front of the hotel. "Should we go in?" I asked.

"Yes," they all answered, and then they were gone.

Is it possible for a man to have his life pass before his eyes and not die? Is our worth in the collective strength of all those who have carried us? They had led me here, back to where I began. Or, if not the precise spot, then another replica in the chain that had somehow survived this long. A hiding place that would soon be swarmed by whichever side happened to win. My helpers had kept me alive long enough to teach me how to desire life. And now they had left me, like a newborn on a doorstep, with no idea how to survive beyond the decision to just keep breathing.

The hotel stood solid as a mausoleum after a flood. It was bold and square, a proud fortress. A sign had blown up against the front steps announcing the grand opening of a now-destroyed department store. The picture was a mixture of gleam and grime. "Be the first," the copy line read, "and you won't have to worry about being the last." I kicked a hole in the sign and opened the front door.

A chain. A series of hotels. Used as barracks. Camouflage. Mc.'s words rang through and at last true in my mind. The reception desk was in the same spot, the furniture and the arrow pointing toward the bar. All slightly different. A little older, younger, identical as twins until you see them side by side.

There were signs of sudden departure. A few emptied weapons. A SAPI vest. A rucksack. In a back booth in the bar, a dead soldier, his gun in front of him, and another man in a bled-through shirt halfway out the service door. I didn't linger long enough to decide who killed whom.

The rooms were even more lush than I'd remembered. There was a claw-foot tub the size of a coffin. Three sinks. A ransacked bed devoid of pillows that only exaggerated the size of the bed. The curtains in this hotel were all sewn to the walls in familiar fashion. Without tearing at them, I could imagine the metal hidden behind them. And behind that the night encroaching like an exhausted army.

I double-locked the door, laughing at the futility, entered the bathroom, and showered in the dark. I dug a leftover soap as deep into my wounds as composure would allow, feeling the bright spike of a pass-out more than once. Die in the shower, I laughed at myself. That'll show them.

Lacking towels, I wrapped myself in a bed sheet to dry, then finally turned on the light. Ten years, that was my guess, and these things are always a guess: my face had added ten years in the couple of months since I'd first checked in. The circles under my eyes were dark as eggplants, with my green irises as the stems. My corneas looked fractured for all the scratches the air had laced across them. My forehead and cheeks were splotchy and raw as a boy's skinned knees, but they didn't share that youth. Lines of worry and regret that had been hinted at before were now deep as ditches. My lips were split from thirst, so I attached my mouth to the faucet and let cold water river down my throat and chin, chill my chest. I drank until it felt like drowning. And I was still thirsty.

Whiskers had sprouted in uneven croppings along my jaw, neck, and chin. I found a mini–Dopp kit in the back of a drawer and lathered up, drawing the razor hard and down, waiting for blood. When I was done, tiny kisses of red bloomed on my left cheek and just above my Adam's apple. I splashed aftershave over them, the sting and scent reminding me of Y. and his Aqua Velva. "Sorry, Y.," I said to the air. I touched my throat where I had taken him out, and regret added to the choke. "I'm sorry," I managed to say, tilting my head up just enough to make it look like a prayer. In case anyone was watching. "Sorry for everything."

I tried to put on my old clothes, but they'd become obsolete. Wrapped in my sheet, I went room to room looking for an outfit. Maybe khakis left behind. A white buttondown. Anything. Mc. had been right. The sevens were suites. But none of the rooms had clothes left behind. Someone had already come through and emptied all the closets, splintered all the drawers.

As I stood in 307, the suite suddenly became too small. The walls and ceiling seemed to quake at the thunder of an approaching silence. The silence that comes after the screaming is over. I didn't want to be buried alive, trapped by plaster and snake-wrapped in wires. I wanted to see the bullet coming, the arc of the arrow, kiss the flame before it swallowed me whole.

The roof-access door had the international warning symbol for "Emergency Only," and I figured I'd finally earned that status. Yet the alarm was mute as I staggered out onto the rooftop. From seventeen floors up, all the waste-land below seemed brighter than the surface of the moon. There were a couple of pipe housings that might have offered momentary shelter when the attack came, but my time and space had ended. Legs and lungs burned like last charcoal, and I battled for breath in the ruined flux. All I had left to do was wait.

Maybe in the end, it was all snapshots and blood clots. No flow, only incidents with the edges cut off. I had missed my life only to find it too late to use it. I was rich with noth-ing left to buy. Not even time. The night fell asleep in the arms of the day, and, wrapped in my sheet, wingless and worried, I pinned my eyes shut and dreamed of dying.

They're here now. It's morning, and I can hear them con-templating action and access points just outside the door. The slow hurry of loading bullets echoes out onto the roof. Jumping suddenly seems a satisfying possibility. At least, for a moment, I could fly. Up away from all the punishment of myself, to land in the graveyard that this war has already dug for me. But somehow, as I peep over the side, I don't want to disappear down at all. I long to fly up. To vanish in clouds and purity, somewhere above all this no, into an impossible possible yes.

But men don't fly up. We only fall down. And now is my time. The time to end all the time I have wasted. All these things I will never know. And the door opens.

They are soldiers, of course, seven, with guns aimed and confusion on their faces. Maybe that they've chased all this way to find a man wrapped in a sheet. Barefoot. Like I am late for a meeting. So late I forgot my shoes. Not a soldier at all. Or at least not a threatening soldier. Just a man trapped at the far edge of his life.

Two of the men are dark-skinned. One with an elegant, African face, totemic. The other short and maybe Latino, his shining face as pinched down as if something fell on it. They speak to each other in broken English and stutter-step my way.

The uniforms. That's it. Familiar. But not green. Beige, with different shoulder patches. The five men behind look eager to shoot, but, with their commanders in front, they'll have to wait until I run or the leaders say bang. Involuntarily, I tense in anticipation of a bullet, and they stop and crouch as if expecting a gun.

"No, no," I say, "I'm unarmed," instantly regretting it. It is obvious. My thin cotton layer hides no weapon, but I don't want to be taken in, arrested for treason, locked away anywhere they choose. I want to die up here. Maybe I will jump.

They stand again, and the front two make it within fifteen feet. I begin to shake. My last dance, I laugh to myself. And they laugh, too. That's how they get through such an execution, I guess. They laugh. So it feels less real.

"Shoot me," I say. "Everyone. At once. That's all I ask." And then the laughter really comes. The African soldier takes in my English slowly, then rolls out a laugh that would seem loud at a party. The others fall in behind. Not dying at the hands of these hyenas, I decide, and I hop up onto the ledge.

"Wait," they say in delayed unison. "No. Come here."

"I'm not going anywhere. I'm already home." I turn and stare down. Ready to step out and free.

"Sir," the small face says to me. "Sir, please, stepping down." I don't step down, just peer back over my shoulder. The other soldiers have laid down their weapons and opened their hands like fathers who have pushed their child too far out on a swing.

"Is this America?" I plead.

"Yes."

"I'm an American," I say, embarrassed, relieved. "Why are we fighting? What happened here?"

"Does it matter?" From one of the crew cuts in back. He speaks out of rank, but everyone knows he's right.

"Look. At our uniforms," the African says. I do, and the familiarity ebbs toward knowledge. "We are peacekeepers. The fighting. It is over." He is now inches from taking my hand and guiding me down.

"No. It's not over." He doesn't know the horrors I know. The bones upon which we are standing. Yet his kindness, his open expression and fistless palm extended, make me utterly weak. I cannot fight as he takes my hand, leads me back onto the roof. The soldiers surround me, pull at me, part comfort, part patting me down for hidden weapons.

"We secured the perimeter this a.m., sir." The African speaks as if singing. "We almost didn't check the roof."

"Sergeant bet the place was abandoned," the Latin man says. "Happy, lost that bet."

"The war," I say.

"The city is secure," one answers.

"Don't have to be afraid."

"Anymore," from another.

"How long you been up here?"

I look at myself in response to his expression. The sheet is smeared with soot. My hands and feet are filthy from rainwater and the rooftop's melted tar. Hunger crawls from my belly out into the whole of me. I touch my face and whiskers surprise my fingers. "I don't know." Maybe I've been asleep for days.

"Where is your family?"

"All gone," I say, tears finding their surface.

"Condolences, sir. But here you are." For a moment, everyone is sad for me, this strange man on the roof. Cigarettes are offered, taken. I look at the spot I almost jumped from and feel like I may have tricked Mc. after all.

"There's nothing left out there," one says, surveying the erased landscape.

"How in the world," the Latin man asks, "did you survive?"

My answer surprises even my mouth. "I decided. To live."

As we begin to walk, hesitantly, like friends who hate good-byes, I put my hand on the Latin soldier's shoulder. "Where are you from? Your accent. Can I ask?"

"The Algarve," he explains.

"I don't know."

"Portugal," he answers. "It is the most beautiful."

He opens the emergency-exit door, allowing me to go first. I step down the stairwell, and the light hits me immediately. And the sound. The sound of soldiers tearing open all the curtains. Every step down takes me deeper into the side-splashing light. "Thank you for coming so far," I say. "To help."

"We all live in the same neighborhood." I pull him into a

half hug as we walk down the stairs, this unexpected friend who came such a distance to find me. Reel me back in. On the second flight of stairs, we come across a dead body, face down. Two of the peacekeepers lift him out of the way, turning him over as we pass. I turn, trying not to look at any more death. It was a body I hadn't seen on my walk up to the roof.

"Yeah, 'cause this asshole was shooting at us."

"'Peacekeeper,'" the African says. "Shouted it to him 'bout a thousand times."

He is dead. No question. As I finally look at the dead man's face, for a flash, it's Mc., winking at me, playing gone again. But then it's simply the blank face of another man who has shed his skin and slipped away. Another man with a gun who discovered it wasn't enough. Mc. is still out there, I can sense it. Telling his stories poorly. Brilliantly. If only to himself.

"Good luck he never make it to the roof," says the African. "Probably shoot you too."

"Nah, me?" I laugh, because he is so right. "I'm bulletproof."

We're nearly all the way down when I finally remember the question. This is one thing I won't die without knowing. "Portuguese," I say loudly, already grateful. "What does *hoje* mean?

"*Hoje*." He corrects my pronunciation.

"*Hoje*. It's a beautiful word." I feel like saying it over and over until the meaning teaches itself to me.

"It is," he agrees. "The most."

"Will you tell me what it means?" But as we reach the mezzanine, and I can see the open hotel door inhaling the morning bright, somehow I already know, before he even answers the question.

ACKNOWLEDGMENTS

My sister, Kristyn Komarnicki, for insight both literary and spiritual, and whose life reminds me daily about sacrificial love.

Heather Zicko, first eyes and last support. A true genius of friendship.

Sergeant First Class Promotable Todd V. Jackson, for details from the field and courage beyond the call.

Dick and Jeannette Seaver, for their resolute dedication and tireless enthusiasm for literature. Because of them, the world is a better place to read.

Cal Barksdale, for caring about every detail, and always pushing for excellence.

My parents, Marigrace and George Komarnicki, for always inspiring me to seek the truth.

My sister, Robyn Hubbard, a true poet of peace.

My wife, Jane Bradbury, to whom this book is dedicated, for being my haven, my getaway, my home.

And for every soldier willing to trade their life for our liberty, their dreams so that we might find rest. It is not possible to say thank you enough.